HEARTSONG

Center Point
Large Print

Also by Debbie Macomber and available from
Center Point Large Print:

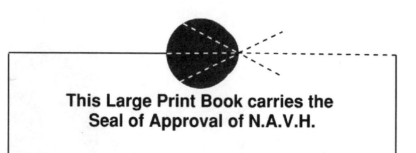

**This Large Print Book carries the
Seal of Approval of N.A.V.H.**

HEARTSONG

Debbie Macomber

CENTER POINT LARGE PRINT
THORNDIKE, MAINE

This Center Point Large Print edition
is published in the year 2012 by arrangement with
Debbie Macomber, Inc.

The text of this Large Print edition is unabridged.
In other aspects, this book may vary
from the original edition.
Printed in the United States of America
on permanent paper.
Set in 16-point Times New Roman type.

ISBN: 978-1-61173-571-0

Library of Congress Cataloging-in-Publication Data

Macomber, Debbie.
Heartsong : a vintage Debbie Macomber novel / Debbie Macomber. —
Center Point large print ed.
p. cm.
ISBN 978-1-61173-571-0 (lib. bdg. : alk. paper)
1. Large type books. I. Title.
PS3563.A2364H45 2012
813'.54—dc23

2012017218

For my parents,
TED AND CONNIE ADLER,
who were afraid that if I used my married name, no one would know I was their daughter.

HEARTSONG

Chapter One

Slowly, silently, the heavy fog began to rise. The brisk offshore breeze set the thick moisture stirring around the Golden Gate Bridge. Gradually the sun broke through the low-lying vapor to display the wonders of the beautiful city of San Francisco.

Releasing a sigh of appreciation for the natural beauty around her, Skye Garvin leisurely strolled toward the hospital. A freshness seemed to flow through her. The demands of teaching a classroom full of enthusiastic kindergartners usually left her physically and mentally drained. But even knowing she would be volunteering several hours at the hospital this afternoon couldn't dampen this new exuberance. The fresh air and brilliant sunlight brought a bounce to her step, and she hummed a catchy tune.

Once on the children's ward she paused to resecure the thick, honey-colored chignon the brisk wind had ruffled about her oval face. Her bright blue eyes sparkled, and her cheeks were whipped a rosy hue.

"You're here at last." Sally Avery, the head pediatric nurse, smiled in greeting. "Billy's been waiting impatiently all afternoon. I think he's ready to collect on his bet."

Skye pulled a wry face. "Oh, dear, I was afraid of that."

The corners of Sally's mouth curved upward. "You realize you're hopeless, don't you? Anyone crazy enough to race that child down the corridor in a wheelchair deserves what she gets."

Skye disguised her own amusement. "Kindly remove that snicker, Sally Avery. How was I to know Billy would practice night and day? You're the one who told me he wouldn't even sit in the wheelchair, and then on the day of the race he takes off like Mario Andretti."

Sally laughed, but her eyes grew serious. "All kidding aside, thank you. I don't know if Billy would ever have voluntarily accepted the wheelchair if it hadn't been for you."

"Oh, nonsense, he just needed a little subtle encouragement," she said, refusing the credit. "I'd better go see the little rascal and discover my forfeit."

"While you're there, see if you can do anything to cheer up his new roommate."

"Okay." Skye paused, thinking she'd detected a gleam of mischief in Sally's expression. "I'll be back with Billy in a few minutes." She flashed a quick smile to the short brunette beside her, who had been her good friend for several years. Skye and Sally were strikingly different in looks, but not temperament. Sally, with her short, stylish curls and slightly plump build, was perpetually dieting, while Skye, tall and slender, never needed to worry about her weight. But both were the impulsive, fun-loving type.

"Good afternoon, Sprout," Skye greeted her favorite ten-year-old.

"Hello, Skye!" Billy's young face lit up with pathetic eagerness. "You haven't forgotten our bet, have you?"

"I doubt that you would let me," Skye said a little dryly.

"You said I could choose anything I wanted."

"Within reason," she added quickly, wondering how she could have been so rash.

"We'd better whisper," Billy warned, and gestured to the hospital bed beside his. The heavy white curtain surrounding the area prevented a look at his new roommate. "He's asleep, I think."

"Then let's go before we wake him," Skye whispered.

"I know what I want for my prize," Billy said loudly, forgetting his own advice in his enthusiasm.

An impatient oath came from the unknown occupant of the room.

"Oops, sorry, Mr. Kiley," Billy apologized.

"Either be quiet or get *out* of here." The hard voice breathed heavily in irritation.

Involuntarily Skye moved closer to Billy. There was no need for the man to be so impatient and brusque. Billy was having a rough enough time. A tragic victim of a hit-and-run driver, he was facing the possibility of spending the rest of his life in a wheelchair. Billy was special, always offering others a ready smile, even when in considerable discomfort. Other children came and left the hospital with amazing dexterity, but Billy had remained for two months, and Skye had become devoted to the courageous youth.

Gently she lifted him into the wheelchair and wheeled him from the room.

"Your new roommate is a man," she said a bit incredulously. No wonder Sally had been so eager for her to meet him. From the beginning of their relationship Sally had assumed the role of matchmaker, intent on finding Skye a husband. Skye usually resigned herself to Sally's schemes but had never allowed any male relationship to develop beyond a light flirtation. Her life would have been so different if only Glen had lived. She immediately cast the unpleasant memories from her mind. It did no good to brood over the might-have-beens in her life.

"Of course Mr. Kiley is a man." Billy said, laughing. "Nurse Sally says he swears like a trooper, and she's right."

"What on earth is he doing on the children's ward?"

"The hospital must be full. I heard someone say my room had the only available bed, but I think Nurse Sally is going to get rid of him fast." His young mouth twisted into a lopsided grin. "Mr.

Kiley threw his lunch tray at the nurse this afternoon."

Skye shook her head disapprovingly. Sally and the other nurses on the children's ward were gentle and patient. They certainly had enough to do without having to deal with an ill-tempered, oversized juvenile.

"It seems your new roommate needs to be reminded of his manners," Skye retorted crisply.

"I don't think you should blame Mr. Kiley for being in a bad mood. He's just in pain and hungry," Billy said with mature insight. "You said for my prize I could have anything I wanted."

"Yes, but—"

"Well, I've decided what I want." He turned in his chair to look at her, his eyes full of boyish enthusiasm. "I want you to get Mr. Kiley to eat. He's only a grouch because he won't let anyone feed him, and his hands are bandaged so he can't feed himself."

"Oh, no, you don't, Billy!" Skye protested, waving her hand back and forth urgently.

"Please, Skye," Billy pleaded. "Remember how you coaxed me? I bet it would work with Mr. Kiley. If anyone can do it, you can."

"Oh, Billy," she sighed, hating to disappoint him. "It just won't work. A man isn't going to get excited over a button that says I Ate the Whole Thing."

Sally joined them in the wide hospital corridor. "Did you tell her yet?" she asked Billy.

"Yeah. I think she'll do it." A reckless grin turned his mouth into a toothless smile.

"No way!" Skye said instantly. "I'm sorry, but your request is beyond reason."

"It sounds fair enough to me," Sally interjected, a glint of laughter shining from her eyes.

"Sally!" Skye glared at her friend, her look speaking volumes.

Unaffected, Sally laughed. "You'd best be on your way, or Billy will be late for his physical therapy session."

"Come on, Skye." Billy's hands hurriedly rotated the large wheels of his chair as he pushed himself toward the elevator. "If we don't hurry, I might be late for dinner."

"And we wouldn't want to miss dinner, would we, Skye?" Sally taunted.

"Come on, you guys," Skye pleaded helplessly.

But Billy refused to be persuaded otherwise, although Skye made repeated attempts as they rode the elevator downward. Leaving him with the physical therapist, she returned to pediatrics.

"I'm glad you're back," Sally said when she saw Skye had returned. "Pastor Johnson phoned and asked if you could visit Mrs. Montressor when you get the chance. There's nothing pressing here. Go now, if you like."

The hospital chaplain often requested that Skye visit certain patients. Her duties entailed reading scripture aloud, writing letters or just visiting with a Christian brother or sister. Mrs. Montressor was a sweet, elderly woman from Skye's church who was being transferred from the hospital to a nursing home after a long illness. Skye realized Mrs. Montressor was a little anxious about the move and just wanted a reassuring chat.

The visit lasted nearly an hour, and Skye returned to pediatrics only a few minutes before Billy was due, so she hurried to put his bed in order. Nervously she entered the room. The curtain around his roommate's bed was open, but his face was turned away from her. She said a quick prayer that she wouldn't wake him and worked as quietly as possible.

"Well, if it isn't little Miss Pollyanna." A gruff voice thick with amusement spoke as she completed making the bed. A grin twisted the corners of his mouth as he regarded her volunteer uniform. He paused to read the button attached below her name tag, which said: I BELIEVE IN MIRACLES.

"Mr. Grinch, I presume," she said with-out her usual warm smile, hoping to show her disapproval of his behavior.

Their gaze met and held as they exchanged looks. Cool arrogance returned her study. As Billy had explained, his hands were bandaged in thick white gauze resembling makeshift boxing gloves; his left arm was propped at an awkward angle in traction. He wasn't strikingly handsome, but was compelling, with a sense of self-assurance. His eyes were a deep gray, widely set and lent his face a look of intensity. His jawline, proud and strong, was ruggedly carved.

His eyes darkened menacingly under her scrutiny, as if he deeply resented her or anyone seeing him disabled. Not that it was likely she would view this unnerving male as weak. He exuded an easy strength and confidence, but Skye could sense his frustration and impatience.

His helplessness stirred something within her, and she suddenly realized she wanted to help this man, but common sense quickly intervened. He was out of her league, and there was little she could do.

Their gazes remained locked until Sally wheeled Billy into the room.

"Okay, young man, let's get you into bed; dinner is on the way." Reverting her attention to Billy's roommate, Sally added, "And, Jordan Kiley, you'll be pleased to know you're being transferred to another ward first thing in the morning."

Amusement returned to the intense gray eyes. "Couldn't wait to be rid of me, could you?" his husky voice challenged.

"Certainly pediatrics will miss your wit and charm," Sally lied, and Billy giggled.

"Just as long as we understand each other." The voice fit the man; low-pitched and demanding. "And as for dinner, either give me something I can eat myself, or forget it. I'm not a baby, and I won't be hand-fed."

Billy's eye quickly caught Skye's, and she shrugged her shoulders in a gesture of defeat, but Billy's eyes widened imploringly.

The large cafeteria cart had arrived from the kitchen, and glancing from the hall to her patient, Sally said, "I'll see what I can do, but it's doubtful."

Skye tucked Billy's sheet in and brought the vanity around from the side of the bed before leaving the room.

"Where are you going, Pollyanna?" Jordan asked.

His question surprised her. "I'll be back," she promised, and offered him a tentative smile.

"Remember, I want to collect on my bet *tonight!*" Billy shouted after her.

The dinner trays had all been delivered . . . save one. Skye stood beside the large cart deep in thought. She knew Jordan Kiley represented a far greater challenge than any child she had ever worked with. It wouldn't be easy to spoon-feed him and salvage his pride at the same time.

"Hello, Skye. I haven't seen you in a while." Joyce Kimball, one of the younger high school volunteers, addressed her warmly. "Do you like the new me?" She turned, allowing Skye to study her appearance. It was unmistakably the Karen Kane look. The sleek, high-fashion model image was sweeping the country. It seemed everyone was imitating the famous beauty: the Karen Kane hairstyle, the Karen Kane designer jeans, the Karen Kane cosmetics.

Skye's eyes widened as an idea began to form. "Joyce," she cried, "you're a genius." Obeying the impulse, Skye began pulling the large pins from her hair.

Several minutes later the latest Karen Kane imitator approached Billy's room. The top button of her uniform was unfastened. Silky, honey-blond curls cascaded over her shoulder. Normally Skye applied her makeup modestly, but now her mouth was liberally coated with a deep red gloss, and blush had been added to accentuate the natural color of her rosy cheeks.

She found Billy enjoying his meal and cast him a secret smile. His jaw dropped at the sight, but he returned her wink in silent communication.

Jordan watched dispassionately as she set the dinner tray on the vanity and rolled it to the side of his bed.

His gaze traveled leisurely over her face, measuring her. Skye's face grew hot under his slow appraisal; her courage nearly failed her.

"You must really believe in miracles if you think I'm going to let you feed me," he announced caustically, sending a shiver of apprehension up her spine.

The words seemed lodged in her throat as his look penetrated through her.

"I learned a long time ago that when it comes to miracles I have to pray as if everything depended on God—and work as if everything depended on me." She was surprised at how composed she sounded.

"Just how do you propose to work *this* miracle?" He sounded cynical.

"I'm prepared to offer you a little inducement."

His thick brows arched in curiosity.

She offered him a warm smile. "You must understand, the nurses are held to a certain code of ethics. But I'm not a nurse, I'm a volunteer." Slowly the moist tip of her tongue circled the glossed lips in a suggestive movement. "I'm prepared to offer you a small reward if you let me feed you."

His eyes showed interest. "What kind of reward?"

Demurely she lowered her long lashes and whispered huskily, "More of a dessert."

Interpreting his silence as consent, she rolled the vanity closer to the bed and dipped the fork into the potatoes. But Jordan's mouth remained defiantly shut, his dark eyes brooding.

Skye's spirits sank; her ploy wasn't going to fool this intuitive male.

Unexpectedly a faint smile formed at the corner of his mouth. "Feed me," he sighed with self-derision. "I always was a sucker for a pretty face."

Her thick lashes fluttered down to conceal the triumph from her expressive blue eyes.

Jordan continued to watch her, his eyes sharp

and intent. Skye knew it was all Billy could do to keep from applauding.

"Do you find fulfillment in life as a hospital volunteer?" Jordan asked between bites.

"I'm responsibly employed. As a matter of fact I hold a highly respected position."

His smile brought a marked defensiveness to her voice. "As it happens, I enlighten, train and discipline."

"She's a kindergarten teacher," Billy supplied laughingly.

"I also button coats, pour juice and kiss away hurts. . . ." Again she was interrupted by Billy.

"She's not married, either."

"Billy!" Skye snapped, her cheeks flushed crimson.

"It happens that way sometimes," Jordan explained to Billy. "She's pretty enough but has probably been jilted or hurt. It'll take time before she's ready to love again." It was an open dare for Skye to contradict him.

Instead she laughed lightly, shrugging off the challenge. "I see that the psychiatrist is *IN*. Thank you for your analysis, doctor." The curve of her mouth softened into a smile.

His gray eyes held her look; he seemed to know she would not be easily provoked.

Now it was her turn to satisfy her curiosity. Putting down the fork, she asked, "How did you manage to get yourself into this fine mess?"

"Car accident." He sounded annoyed, but his anger wasn't directed at Skye but at himself. "Besides totaling my car I managed to ruin my first vacation in years."

"What happened?" she asked, chilled by the memory of another accident long ago.

"Lombard Street." He groaned at his own stupidity. "I'd heard so much about San Francisco's famous curved street and decided to take it as fast as possible. I didn't make the last curve—I guess I'd had one beer too many."

Skye had read an account of the accident in the morning paper. The crazy fool was lucky not to have been killed—or to have killed someone else. Lombard Street, with eight consecutive turns at ninety-degree angles, was difficult to maneuver at the best of times. "Did you enjoy the novelty of reading about yourself this morning?" she asked, hiding her disapproval of such irresponsible behavior.

Some emotion flickered from his eyes, and for a brief second Skye thought it might be alarm.

"Are you a teacher, like Skye?" Billy interjected his own curiosity.

"No. I work for a radio station."

Billy's voice rose eagerly. "Are you a disc jockey?"

The pause was only momentary. "Among other things," he remarked absently. "You say there was an accident report in the morning paper?"

"Would you like a copy? I'm sure there's an extra paper in the lobby. I can get it if you like."

"Please." He sounded grateful.

Skye returned a few minutes later with a section of the paper. It was only a short account of the accident, a few sentences that didn't even give his name.

Jordan seemed to relax and joked. "What does a man have to do in this town to get his name in the paper?"

Gently Skye placed her hand on his arm. "Has your family been contacted?"

The slant of Jordan's mouth became cynical. "As there is only my mother, I can't see much point in distressing her over a few scratches."

A badly broken arm could hardly be considered a scratch. Nonetheless, Skye laughed lightly. "Obviously the poor man has been jilted, Billy. He just hasn't learned to trust again. Or as Sally would say—you're either gay, divorced or just plain unmarriageable."

"At thirty-six, I suspect she's right." But Jordan didn't enlighten her into which category he fit.

Betty Fisher, Billy's mother, arrived as Billy finished his meal, and she wheeled her son into the large recreation-visiting room at the end of the hall.

"You coming, Skye?" Billy asked, eager for her to join the children and play the piano.

"Not until later; I'll only be a few minutes," she promised.

Giving Jordan the last bit of his dinner, she asked, "Now, that wasn't so bad, was it?"

"When do I get dessert?" The inflection of his low voice said he wasn't asking about the apple pie.

"Soon," she lied. "I'll take your tray to the cart and be right back."

Skye lingered outside the room for several seconds gathering her courage. The I ATE THE WHOLE THING button was clenched tightly in the palm of her hand. Unsteady fingers looped a long strand of honey-blond hair behind her ear. Jordan Kiley wasn't going to find humor in her little deception.

His eyes probed her as she entered, but she purposely avoided eye contact with him.

"I didn't think you would come back." His voice was cool.

"Of course I was coming back. I always keep my promises," she said, finding it difficult to resume her charade. "Now, close your eyes," she whispered seductively, and bent over him.

He complied, surrounding her lithe form with a bandaged arm.

For a fleeting second Skye considered kissing him, but quickly shut her mind to the temptation. Instead she attached the button to his hospital gown and easily slipped from his arm.

Jordan caught his breath and lunged for her. The attempt to catch her was ludicrous, and Skye stood only inches from his reach, her blue eyes triumphant. A certain pride at having outwitted him prompted her mouth to curve into an irritating Mona Lisa smile.

Jordan grinned suddenly; all signs of anger were quickly erased from his features. "Clever trick, Pollyanna, but have no doubts I will collect what is due me."

Skye flushed a deep red. He was the type of man who ultimately got what he wanted, but his words were more of a promise than a threat. Disguising the effect of his words, she put on a smiling facade and made busy work of fastening the button of her uniform while gaining control of her racing heartbeat. "We'll see about that," she said with far more confidence than she was feeling.

Gradually the tension began to fade, and she relaxed. Combing her fingers through her long hair she said, "Good-bye, Mr. Grinch."

The sound of his low laugh followed her into the corridor.

She had escaped Jordan Kiley this time, but she realized she wouldn't be so fortunate a second time.

Billy and his mother, along with the other children and their visitors, were waiting for Skye when she entered the recreation room. An upright mahogany piano rested against the outside wall, and when she sat on the padded bench, the happy chatter grew silent.

Skye's slim fingers flew across the ivory keys in a light, catchy tune, and soon the small audience was clapping in beat to the happy melody. The uplifting beat of the music eased some of the worry etched so clearly on the faces of the children and their families. It was for this reason Skye came week after week, year after year. If she could help others forget their own unhappiness, even for a short while, then her time was well spent.

Although everyone enjoyed the piano playing, it was the songs Skye composed that the children loved the best. The clever verses of make-believe dragons, castles and children's dreams brought smiles and giggles to happy cherubic faces.

Skye's closing number was a soft lullaby she had composed using Psalm sixty-two:

> My soul finds rest in God alone;
> my salvation comes from Him.
> He alone is my rock and salvation;
> He is my fortress, I will never be shaken.
> Find rest, O my soul, in God alone;
> my hope comes from Him.

Rich and melodious, her voice rang clear and true through the passageway, and as she hummed the final notes several children yawned, ready for sleep. Hoping to place the homesick child in a familiar family routine, the hospital encouraged each parent to put his or her child to bed before leaving.

As Betty wheeled Billy toward his room she asked Skye hopefully, "Do you have time for a cup of coffee tonight?" Alone and young, Betty Fisher needed someone as a sounding board for her worries over Billy's uncertain future.

"I always have time for you, Betty," Skye assured the young mother.

"Are you coming tomorrow, Skye?" Billy asked the same question after every visit, as if he were afraid she would disappear someday, just as his father had done.

"No, Sprout, but I'll be here Thursday," she whispered, hoping not to wake Jordan. The white curtain had been replaced, and the nurse had put a finger to her lips when they had entered the room, indicating Jordan was asleep. Skye had given an unconscious sigh of relief.

Just as Betty and Skye were ready to kiss Billy good night, Sally stuck her head in the door. "Do you need a ride home tonight, Skye?"

"Not tonight, thanks, Sally."

"Okay, I'll see you Thursday."

"Good night, Sally." She smiled a friendly farewell. "Sleep tight, Sprout," she whispered tenderly, and lovingly kissed his brow.

Halfway across the darkened room a clear male voice taunted, "Good night, Pollyanna."

Chapter Two

School didn't go well the next day. Skye had difficulty concentrating on her teaching and several times found her troubled thoughts drifting to Jordan Kiley. In the light of the new day she felt no sense of triumph over her deception or in having bested him, only a guilty uneasiness. Not that she was worried he would collect his "dessert," as he had threatened. Sally had mentioned Jordan was being transferred to another ward as soon as possible and probably would be discharged by Friday. There was little likelihood she would ever see him again. Then why did this restless feeling persist?

Skye welcomed three thirty and the dismissal of her kindergartners. The confused day hadn't been all her doing. There were only a few days left before spring break, and anticipating the vacation, the class seemed restless and over-active.

It was after four when she finally left the school for home. Her apartment, a rare find in the Marina district, had large bay windows that presented a sweeping panorama of the Pacific waters. Healthy, abundant plants hung in the window, flourishing under her tender care and in the warmth of the reflected sun. It was a homey apartment, decorated with cushioned rattan furniture, and possessed the appeal of simplicity.

The lock on her front door clicked loudly as she turned the key; then she paused momentarily to replace the key inside her purse.

"Howdy, neighbor." The apartment door across the hall opened at the sound.

"Hello, John." She gave him a deliberate, casual smile. "Nice day, isn't it?" She didn't wait for his reply before pushing open her door.

"No need to rush inside, Sweet Stuff. I've been wanting to talk to you. We're neighbors; we should get to know each other better."

"Not today," Skye offered apologetically but firmly. The last thing she wanted was to become trapped in John Dirkson's apartment for the rest of the afternoon. Strikingly handsome and charming, John didn't lack female companionship, but Skye found his sleek good looks and huge ego unattractive. Unfortunately, because of his vanity he refused to accept her rebuffs as sincere; her refusal to become another notch on his bedpost made her a novelty.

"It's not going to work, you know," John said, affecting disinterest.

"What's not going to work?"

He hooked his thumb lazily on the belt loop of his designer jeans and leaned against the open door frame. "This playing hard to get."

"I'm so pleased to hear it." She adopted a

lighthearted, bright smile. "I was worried for a minute."

"I'll get you yet," he added confidently, not in the least discouraged by her attitude.

"No, you won't," she said quickly, then stepped inside her apartment and firmly closed the door.

She placed her purse and mail on the entryway table and hung her beige poplin coat in the closet. After slipping off her pumps, she walked barefooted into the tiny kitchen to put on water to boil for tea. Obeying habit, she turned on the radio in her bedroom while changing clothes. The air was crisp and chilly, and she chose a winter outfit that had been a birthday gift from her brother. The red plaid pants slipped easily over her slim hips, and the mock turtleneck sweater was in striking contrast to her golden hair.

A slow and soothing romantic ballad filled the room. Unbidden, the music conjured up a mental image of Jordan's taunting smile, and Skye bit into her lower lip, nibbling on it unconsciously.

"Go away," she said aloud, and irritably turned off the radio.

A few minutes later she stood before the bathroom mirror, pulling the pins from her hair.

"Rapunzel . . . Rapunzel . . . let down your hair," she laughed, and wondered at her strange mood. The thick curls shimmered down like liquid gold upon her shoulders and back. Its length was a nuisance; a shorter style would have been far more practical, but she couldn't summon the courage to have it cut. Glen had always loved her long, thick hair, and in her own way, its length was a symbolic memory of his love. She brushed the curls vigorously until they crackled with electricity. On impulse she left it down, the length shaping attractively about her shoulders. In reality she was much too tall to be wearing it up all the time, but she had long ago quit worrying about her height. Accustomed to seeing her hair away from her face, she did an automatic double take, surprised at how good she looked, when she happened to glance in the mirror on her way out the door.

The teapot was whistling, and soon the aroma of cinnamon and spice perfumed the air. The mail contained a newsy letter from her mother in Florida, and Skye sat with her cup of tea, propping her feet on the large wicker chest that served as a coffee table, before immersing herself in the letter.

She needed this time to relax and unwind from her day but instead found herself fidgety and restless. Perhaps she should do some shopping and even splurge and have a meal out before attending the Wednesday evening church service and choir practice.

The idea proved to be a good one. She bought herself a new pair of shoes; simple but comfortable ones she could wear to school. Impulsively she stopped in a toy store to browse around. Billy had been so unselfish in his choice of a prize that she picked out a small electronic game he was sure to enjoy. Since it was on sale, it was easy to rationalize the expense.

Pleased with her purchases, Skye decided to deliver Billy's gift to him instead of waiting until the following evening. And while she was at the hospital maybe Sally would join her for a light meal in the cafeteria.

As usual pediatrics was a hub of activity. Nurses and the other staff members moved with purpose. Skye stopped by the nurses' station to leave a message for Sally, then lightheartedly headed for Billy's room.

Entering the room, she froze midstep. Billy's bed was empty, but Jordan Kiley was very much present. The force of his personality filled the room, compelling and totally male. He viewed her shock with a half-smile that touched the corner of his mouth.

Suddenly the smile left his eyes, and he grimaced as his rugged face twisted with pain. Her surprise quickly receded into concern and she haphazardly deposited her packages on Billy's empty bed before rushing to Jordan's side.

"What's the matter? Should I get a nurse?" Alarm thickly coated her voice.

Before she could protest, she found herself roughly jerked against the side of the bed. The strength of his right arm was unbelievable, and the unyielding muscles of his upper arm flexed as he held her firmly in check. A slow, satisfied grin spread evenly across his face.

Panic erupted within Skye but it was useless to struggle against his superior strength. Frantically she whispered, "Please, don't."

Jordan studied the terror in her eyes, and gradually his merciless grip relaxed, but his bandaged hand remained around her waist.

"This is just to let you know I can claim what is mine any time I want. No more games, Pollyanna."

Numbly Skye nodded; her voice seemed to be locked in her throat, and she was breathing unevenly.

His arm fell, freeing her. "You're really frightened, aren't you? Has it been so long since a man kissed you that you tremble at the possibility?" His voice was smooth and mocking.

"Of course not," she denied stiffly, backing away from him. Her hands were still shaking when she bumped against the rail of Billy's bed. "I brought this for Billy," she said, her hands groping for the smaller package. "Would you see that he gets it?" she asked in what she hoped sounded like a normal voice.

Jordan ignored her request, his eyes studying her astutely. "You've been badly hurt, haven't you?" His words were soft with discernment. "How long have you managed to hide behind that easy laugh and witty personality?"

In spite of herself Skye's head snapped up, and what color remained quickly drained from her face. His perceptions were unnerving. Automatically she swallowed back a denial; as for her quick wit, where was it when she needed it so desperately?

"I should have remembered Billy wouldn't be here," she said, ignoring his question. It was a struggle to keep her voice even. "Please tell him I'll be back later."

"Oh, no, you don't," Jordan interjected quickly. "I'm not letting you go now, not when I pulled every string I know to remain on this floor until I got the chance to see you again."

His disclosure halted Skye's flight from the room. "You wanted to see me again?" she asked incredulously. Slowly a smile meandered across her face as she realized what he was saying. "Ah, you just wanted to collect your dessert."

He answered with a lazy grin. "True, but thinking of a way to even the score helped pass the long day." He shifted slightly and grimaced with a rush of pain. "Darn this arm," he swore harshly.

Again Skye found his discomfort greatly affecting her, but she forced herself to stay where she was. "That trick won't work a second time," she said, although she realized his pain was genuine.

"Pity," he murmured with a forced smile.

"Is there something I can do?"

"No, it'll pass in a moment." His breathing was hard and labored.

"Please," she whispered, her gaze resting on his strong face. "Let me do something to help." The compassion he evoked in her was almost physical. "I'll get a nurse."

"No," he shouted with sudden violence.

His anger shocked her, and she stepped back as if burned.

Jordan made a savage gesture. "I didn't mean to snap your head off, but the nurses can do nothing." He relaxed against the pillow, the pain easing. "The doctors placed a pin in my arm, and every now and then a pain shoots through it like fire." His eyes darkened defiantly. "But I refuse to be constantly drugged."

Skye's legs felt shaky; it was ridiculous to be so affected by this man.

"Skye," he said, using her name for the first time. "Will you stay awhile?"

"I . . . can't." Nervously she moistened her dry lips. "I'm meeting Sally for dinner." She had only left a message for Sally to meet her if she could, but Skye knew if she were to remain with Jordan she would betray the unsettling effect he had upon her.

His mouth tightened, and his eyes narrowed.

Too late, Skye realized she had injured his arrogant male pride. Jordan wasn't the kind of man women would easily refuse. She had already tried his vanity before with her deception; to provoke him again would be unwise.

"Afraid?" he mocked.

"No, of course not," she denied instantly.

"How about later tonight then?" he said, surprising her by pursuing the subject.

"I don't think so. . . . I sing with the church choir, and we practice on Wednesday nights," she hurried to explain. She was making a mess of this. Her whole purpose as a Christian and a hospital volunteer was to help others. Surely it went against his nature to even ask her to stay and she knew she was denying him only because of the strange feelings he stirred within her. It was wrong, and she felt guilty. "I suppose I could stop for a few minutes afterward, but it might be late."

"Don't worry, I'll be awake." He sounded like he was silently laughing at her.

"It's spring vacation next week, isn't it?" Sally asked as the late afternoon sunshine filtered through the hospital cafeteria.

"Praise God, yes," Skye rejoiced openly. "I could do with a vacation." Maybe all this turmoil with Jordan was just the result of a bad case of spring fever.

Eyeing Skye's meager dinner, Sally demanded, "How can you survive with just a bowl of soup?"

Skye couldn't very well admit that her confrontation with Jordan had robbed her of all appetite. "I ate a little something before leaving the house." A small deception since she'd had only tea.

Sally pushed the remainder of her salad aside. "I hate dieting," she declared vehemently. "I could kill for a pizza."

Skye couldn't keep from laughing. Sally had been dieting with no real success ever since Skye had known her.

"Losing weight would be easier if you exercised more often," Skye advised with an encouraging smile. "Why not run with me, Sally? It'll help."

Sally rolled her eyes expressively. "Thanks, but no thanks. I'm not that desperate. You've forgotten I've seen you run. I couldn't keep up with you if I was pedaling a bicycle." Absently her hand smoothed a nonexistent crease from the skirt of her uniform. "If you weren't so easy to like, I could be jealous of you."

"Me?" Skye was genuinely shocked. "I can't believe that. I'm the one who steps into a cold apartment every night. I don't have a loving husband or a precious baby like Anne Marie. I should be the envious one."

A full smile teased Sally's mouth. "You don't have twenty extra pounds to lose, either. I guess it's just a case of the grass being greener on the other side of the fence. But honestly, if you're lonely, let me introduce you to Andy's new accountant."

"Sally, no!" Skye interrupted brusquely. "I'm a big girl now and quite capable of finding my own dates."

"Jordan Kiley has been asking questions about you."

"Oh?" Skye took another sip of her coffee, hoping to appear nonchalant and hide her interest.

"You know me," Sally grinned. "By three o'clock in the afternoon I'd sell my soul for a chocolate chip cookie, and Kiley offered me the whole bakery." Her eyes sparkled with impish delight. "I spilled my guts."

"Sally!"

"Oh, all right. I hardly said a word." She paused, mumbling something under her breath.

Skye couldn't let the matter drop. "Pardon me?" she asked firmly.

"I said, I didn't have to say a word. Billy told Kiley everything."

"May the Lord preserve me," Skye groaned.

Glancing at her wristwatch, Sally stood. "I've got to rush, or I'll be late. By the way, Kiley is being transferred to the third floor after dinner. You might stop by and say hello; it's the only way you'll be able to clear away any untruths."

Sally looked surprised at Skye's laugh. "I just might do that." Not for the world would she relate what had happened that afternoon, but by her own admission, she was interested in Jordan Kiley.

Flashing Skye an approving smile, Sally said,

"You should wear the new blue dress we bought not long ago the next time you come. You're quite a knockout in it."

Skye had no such intention and released her breath with feeling. "Yes, Mother."

Unaffected by the heavy sarcasm, Sally laughed. "See you tomorrow."

The church choir was practicing for an Easter cantata, and several members of the group were already present when Skye joined them.

"Here's our little songbird." The male director smiled and handed her the sheet music.

"At five foot ten, I can hardly be described as little," she joked with the ease of familiarity. Others joined in the teasing banter, and the sound of laughter echoed across the empty church.

The practice proceeded with only a few minor interruptions.

Skye's solo came before the final reprise; her rich, clear voice vibrated through the room with brilliant bravura.

"I get chills down my spine every time you sing," Mrs. Peterman, the pianist, said as the choir was dismissed. "Have you ever considered singing professionally, dear?"

Skye had been asked the question before and considered it a supreme compliment. But singing for money was something she'd never consider. She was perfectly content with the uncomplicated pattern of her life, and held no aspirations for fame and glory.

"Some of us are going out for coffee. Will you join us, Skye?" the director asked.

"Not tonight," she apologized ruefully. "I'm visiting a . . . friend." By now she thoroughly regretted the promise she'd made to stop by the hospital. Any contact with Jordan Kiley was asking for trouble, and it would be far better to avoid him.

Walking swiftly to the hospital elevator, Skye didn't consider stopping to visit Billy; it was after nine o'clock, and he was sure to be asleep. Besides, she didn't feel up to Sally's curiosity.

Visiting hours had been over an hour earlier, and since she wasn't well known by the third floor nursing staff, they were sure to ask her to leave after only a few minutes anyway. She sighed in relief and stopped just long enough at the nurses' station to ask Jordan's room number and be sure they knew she was there.

"It's past visiting hours," the nurse informed her disapprovingly after relaying Jordan's room number.

"I know, I'll only be a few minutes," Skye said, and beamed her one of her brightest smiles before starting down the silent corridor. About halfway down raised voices could be heard. The most prominent, deep and rich, rumbled angrily with a cutting edge. It didn't take Skye two seconds to recognize the voice as Jordan's.

"I can see you're up to your persnickety ways, Mr. Grinch." She stood stiffly in the open doorway. Both the nurse and Jordan turned their attention to her. A furrow of painful frustration lined the forehead of the red-faced nurse.

The corner of Jordan's mouth lifted in a half-smile, thawing the cynical curve of his features. "Welcome, Pollyanna."

"Good evening, miss." The nurse flashed Skye a grateful smile. "I'm afraid visiting hours are over." The older woman calmly stepped to Jordan's bed. "But I feel we can make an exception tonight *if* Mr. Kiley can be convinced to accept his medication."

The line of Jordan's mouth tightened in grim disapproval. "I refuse to be blackmailed!" he spat.

"In which case I'll have to ask your friend to leave," the nurse returned just as sharply.

"Good-bye, Jordan." Skye turned away from the door.

A disgusted sound of exasperation came from his throat. "All right, I'll take the darn pill, but I don't like it."

Smiling, Skye unbuttoned her coat and laid it across the chair while the nurse handed Jordan the pill and a glass of water. He had been transferred to a private room. It was spacious and large, containing two comfortably upholstered chairs and an end table with a lamp. Skye wondered at the expense. This was probably the only bed available, and she murmured a silent prayer that his insurance would cover the additional cost.

The nurse winked on her way out the door, and when Skye turned to Jordan, his face was transformed from the heavy scowl to a welcoming grin. Unsteady fingers looped a long curl of hair around her ear.

"You should always leave your hair down, it's lovely," Jordan said, and watched with amusement as color suffused her face.

Why had she ever left it down? It seemed to welcome comment; several people had mentioned it during the course of the evening, and by now she was thoroughly sorry and vowed it would be a long time before she did it again.

"Thank you," she replied stiffly, suddenly self-conscious and unsure. "Are you eating?" Her gaze followed the pattern of the linoleum floor.

"No one has offered me any rewards or desserts." The teasing quality of his voice was a mocking reminder of her game the night before.

Her deep blue eyes crinkled in amusement and bounced away from the strong lines of his face. "Trickery and extortion seem to be the only effective means of dealing with that arrogant pride of yours."

"Ah, but if the food were better, your scheming wouldn't be necessary." His eyes held a dancing light. "What I wouldn't give for a thick pizza and a cold beer."

Skye's gaze was drawn back to him. The light dinner hadn't satisfied her, and now her stomach growled hungrily. "Pizza does sound good, doesn't it?"

"Like heaven," Jordan returned wistfully.

"Italian sausage, mushroom and black olive, covered with a thick layer of mozzarella cheese?"

"Anchovies," Jordan added.

"Okay, but only on your half." She sat, unzipped her boot, and pulled a small, flat plastic card from the bottom of her shoe.

"What are you doing?"

"Getting out the money to pay for the pizza," she replied, as if he were dense.

"What pizza?" He sounded like an amnesia victim.

"The Italian sausage, mushroom and black olive with anchovies on one half pizza—the one I am going across the street to order and sneak inside this room—pizza," she explained in one giant breath.

His rueful smile became a soft chuckle. "Of course, I should have known—*that* pizza."

Skye laughed and limped on one shoeless foot to the door to peek down the hallway.

"Now what are you doing?" he demanded in exasperation.

"Checking the entrance to the stairs. I can't use

the elevator since it opens directly in front of the nurses' station, and the only way I can avoid their eagle eyes is to take the stairs. That wasn't a sleeping pill she gave you by any chance, was it?"

"No, one of those blasted pain killers." Anger reverberated in his husky voice.

Zipping up her boot, Skye smiled reassuringly. "I'll be back before you know it."

"I'll be waiting."

Skye returned in far less time than she expected. She opened the door to Jordan's room and closed it quietly behind her after she hurried inside, hoping to avoid attracting anyone's attention. She was breathing hard from the exertion of running up three flights of stairs.

"That didn't take long." Jordan's head was drawn back, poised and alert.

"They weren't very busy." She set the square cardboard box on the vanity.

"Boy, that smells good," he said, sighing, as she lifted the lid to the steaming pizza. "I think I'll be able to manage on my own if you give me the pieces in a napkin."

"Okay, but if it's awkward, I don't mind feeding you," she offered.

The silence between them was serene as they ate. Skye smiled to herself a couple of times as she watched Jordan's attempts to eat the pizza with his one bandaged hand. Actually he was doing very well, and it surprised her. Perhaps she was making too much of this attraction. What harm would result from a budding friendship? What did she have to fear?

"I hope you won't find me unduly nosy," Jordan said, his voice cutting into her thoughts, "but I was wondering if you always carry your money in your shoe."

"Do you think I have a foot fetish?" she questioned with a laugh, her tone matching the lightness of his. "Actually it's a precautionary measure against muggers."

His thick brows arched.

"San Francisco is one of the most beautiful, romantic cities in the world, but that doesn't make us exempt from crime. I carry several dollar bills in my wallet, and anything larger in my shoe. Brad, my older brother, worries about my living alone and advised me always to carry several dollars in my purse just in case I do get mugged. Then the robber won't beat me in frustration over an empty purse."

"You're kidding."

"No, I'm not," she defended herself. "A girl alone in a big city, even a city as beautiful as San Francisco, is forced into a defensive stance. Crime is a fact of life, and after some of the stories my brother has told me, I'm ready to play it safe."

"Why do you do it then?" he mocked openly.

"Do what?" She glanced up from her pizza.

"Live alone. You're an attractive, enticing

blonde. Surely there's some man standing on the sidelines just waiting for you to say the word."

His inquisitiveness quickly resurrected the defense barrier of humor she hid behind, and she responded with a hearty laugh. "You make my life sound like a football game. I hate to disappoint your curious nature, but there is no one waiting for my punt return."

Jordan raised a dubious brow, but smiled into her laughing eyes. "You think you're pretty smart, don't you?"

"Without a doubt." She wrinkled her nose and fluttered her eyelashes wickedly. She was having a good time, and smiled, unable to remember when she'd enjoyed an evening more. Perhaps she was enjoying it too much.

"It's after ten. I think I'd better go. I'm a working girl, you know, and there would be Hades to pay if I was found out now." She was referring to the nurses.

"I don't want you to leave." A disturbing light in his eyes studied her. "I don't think there are many women in the world who would spend an evening visiting a demanding, ill-tempered invalid."

"There's no need to thank me. I enjoyed it; it's been fun."

"I owe you for the pizza." His expression became strangely brooding, as if it were a great insult against his pride to have her pay for their meal.

"Oh, no, please, it was my treat. You're the one out of work—"

"I can afford a pizza." His mouth twisted angrily.

"I'm sure you can," she sighed, drawing a deep breath. If anything, her insistence was doing more harm than good. Please, her eyes implored, let's not ruin our time by arguing over something so petty.

He flashed her a tender smile, his eyes holding hers magnetically. "You are very lovely."

Her eyes widened in surprise and her heart thundered against her ribs as her mind searched for some witty retort, but it was as if her senses had been struck numb. Self-consciously she lowered her head, the long, golden strands of hair falling forward, wreathing her flushed face. Just a few seconds before they had been teasing and joking; now, disconcertingly, they were on intimate terms.

"Don't, Jordan, please," Skye whispered shakily.

"Why not?" he asked quietly. "You're a beautiful woman, inside and out."

Skye drew a steadying breath and quirked her eyebrows suspiciously. "I thought you broke your arm in the car accident. I didn't realize you had also suffered brain damage. Your tongue may be smooth, Jordan Kiley, but you won't have me believing out and out fantasy. I am no raving beauty." Her voice shook slightly. "Besides being a virtual Amazon, did you happen to notice my schnozzle?" She placed her index finger on the tip of her nose, and crossed her eyes as if examining its extended length.

"Good night, Mrs. Kalabash, wherever you are." With a theatrical gesture typical of Jimmy Durante, Skye stepped across the room where her coat was resting on the chair.

A low, gravelly laugh shook Jordan's shoulders. "Skye—" his laughing, gray eyes suddenly became serious "—come here," he requested softly.

"Not on your life," she retorted.

His round eyes feigned innocence. "You don't trust me?"

"No!" She finished buttoning her coat.

"I'm still hungry," he insisted.

"Then ring for the nurse," she suggested. "The hospital keeps a supply of snacks available."

"I was thinking more along the lines of dessert." He smiled provocatively. "I seem to have developed a sweet tooth lately."

Skye's heart lodged somewhere near her throat at the suggestiveness of his tone. "In which case I suggest you go on a diet," she countered smoothly, belying the uneven beat of her heart.

Jordan chuckled softly. "Good night, my frightened little bird."

It was an accurate description. Her heart hammered fearfully against her ribs like a trapped, wild fledgling. Why she should experience such alarm was a mystery. Jordan Kiley was just a man. Rugged and compelling, but nonetheless a man not unlike a hundred others she had successfully parried in the past years.

"Good night, Jordan," she whispered, quietly closing the door after her.

"Are you coming tomorrow?" he called brusquely.

His sharp question brought her back inside the room. His eyes were directed solely upon her, and she frowned, confused by his barely concealed anger until she understood. His pride resented the necessity of asking her to return. She hovered uncertainly, just long enough for his face to twist into a dark scowl.

Skye found herself incapable of meeting his gaze. "All right," she nodded. "I'm working on the children's ward until about eight. I'll stop in after that."

Jordan nodded. "I'll see you then."

Chapter Three

Everything went better on Thursday. Not that her kindergarteners behaved any differently, Skye realized, but that her attitude had changed. Instead of finding herself constantly on edge, she was more relaxed and at ease with the children.

Skye decided to stay after class and tie up a few loose ends. As part of the educational budget cutbacks the janitor cleaned the classrooms only twice a week. But a high sense of neatness drove her to sweep the floors once or twice a week herself.

After she'd swept and straightened the small desks into even rows, Skye cut out the letters for the bulletin board she had designed for the month of April. There would be plenty of time to do it during vacation week, but she knew she wouldn't rest easy until the project was finished.

She was sitting at her desk cutting jaggedly shaped letters from brightly colored paper when a gruff voice interrupted her. "Need any help, little sister?"

"Brad!" she exclaimed. "What are you doing here?"

"What's the matter, aren't I welcome?" Brad Garvin was a taller version of Skye. Lean and angular, he had blond hair and vivid blue eyes that mirrored those of his sister.

"Of course you are." A certain amount of curiosity entered her eyes. Brad had been unemployed for several weeks, caught in the economic slump of the construction trade. New housing starts were at a record low, and as a carpenter, things didn't look promising. But from the smile on his face whatever news he had must be good.

"I tried to phone you last night, but you weren't home. Don't tell me you were on some hot date?"

"You're right, I'm not telling," she teased lightly, and threw a dusting cloth at his mocking grin. Five years separated them, but throughout their youth and into adulthood they had remained close and good friends.

Without so much as a flinch Brad neatly caught the rag. "Be careful, little sister, I could pull the pins from your hair."

"Promises, promises, promises." A smile lit up her face. "If you weren't so infuriating, I'd admit it was good to see you. What have you been up to?"

"Not much." He sat on her desk, one leg dangling over the edge. "I talked to Mom last night. Moving in with Aunt Vi has been great for her. Janey is counting the shopping days left until her ninth birthday and, oh, Peggy's pregnant."

"Pregnant?" Skye breathed in disbelief; her blue eyes widening. "You're not teasing, are you?"

Brad and Peggy had given up hope of having

another child even though the doctors assured them there was no medical reason for their difficulties. Certainly Janey, born a year after their wedding, proved they were capable of having children.

Brad didn't need to answer her doubts, his laughing blue eyes said it all.

With a burst of joy Skye stood and enthusiastically hugged her brother. "Oh, Brad, I'm so pleased. When is the baby due? How is Peggy feeling? Is Janey happy?"

"Slow down. One question at a time." He laughed at her enthusiasm.

"You've had time to get used to the idea, and don't tell me you weren't just as excited when Peggy told you." A knowing look flashed from her eyes.

Brad shook his head. "I'm still having trouble believing it. We've tried so hard for so many years, and now, when we can least afford it and haven't got a penny of insurance, Peggy gets pregnant."

"Listen, count your blessings. Wasn't it you who told me God's timing is always perfect? Besides, if you need help . . ."

"No," he said, raising his voice with pride. "Don't even offer, Skye. You've done enough for us already. The baby's not due until January, and I'm sure to have found some kind of employment by then."

"All right, but I'm going to pray up a storm. . . . Remember, the effective prayer of a righteous *woman* availeth much."

"That seems to be a slight misquote of that verse. But for heaven's sake, don't let that stop you: pray!

"By the way, where were you last night?" he insisted again.

"Out." She batted her eyelashes wickedly. It wasn't like her to hold back anything from her brother, but to explain about Jordan would be pointless. Skye had decided not to see him again, and with the decision came a relaxed freedom. Jordan had the uncanny power to stir in her feelings she had long considered dead. He was too astute, too perceptive. Her simple defenses would easily crumble under the force of his personality. The uncomplicated pattern of her life suited her, and there was no reason to openly invite disruption.

Playfully her tightened fist punched his upper arm. "A baby after all these years. You had it in you after all, you big brute."

Brad was a wonderful husband and father. He had been a solid rock supporting her in a dark world after Glen's death. If anyone deserved happiness, it was Brad.

The children's ward was bustling with predinner rush, and after a hasty visit with Billy and Sally,

Skye resumed her volunteer duties. The singing followed dinner. Several of the children dissolved into fits of laughter over Skye's cleverly worded jingles. Cheers and applause filled the recreation room as parents and staff joined the merriment. Skye's own elated mood became infectious, and even the most cynical could not help being drawn in and touched by the joy shining from the eyes of the children.

Her closing number was one that held deep meaning for Skye. She had composed it herself, and it spoke of darkness and light, of sorrow and joy, the contrast between the valley and the mountain top. The final words brought huge smiles of awe and appreciation from the audience.

> Don't let the song escape from your
>   life
> For every life must have a song
> A song to ring out loud and long
> Let Jesus be your heartsong.

"Sometimes I think I know you so well, Skye Garvin, and then there are times like these and I realize I don't know you at all." Sally looked at Skye, her brow marred by a puzzled frown.

"What makes you say that?" Skye questioned.

"I'm not exactly sure. The quality of your voice when you're especially happy." She shrugged her shoulders. "There are times I have the impression that one reason you are able to communicate so well with these families is that you've walked through some deep valley yourself. And yet you're so outgoing and positive, it's almost as if you've never known a minute's worry." They slowly continued down the hall. "Like Betty Fisher." Sally paused. "There's a communication, an understanding between you that's beyond compassion."

If Sally was seeking confidences, Skye wasn't going to share them. Glen, his death and all that followed afterward, was in the past. Reliving those terrible months would be like tearing open a half-healed wound. And yet Sally was her friend, and she didn't wish to offend her.

"Things are not always as they appear," Skye admitted cryptically. "But I do know that one has to walk through the valley to know the exultation of a mountaintop."

Sally looked far from appeased but changed her line of questioning. "What did you bring for dinner?" she asked. "Yogurt and sunflower seeds again?" she teased lightly, and added, "I certainly hope you're not planning to wear that outfit to visit Jordan Kiley."

"What?" Skye exploded. "Who said I was visiting him?" Her suspicions immediately bobbed to the surface. How like Jordan to try and outwit her. He must have guessed she would change her mind and back out of her promise.

But involving Sally seemed underhanded and unfair.

"*You* said you were visiting him."

"I most certainly did not," Skye denied hotly.

"It seems to me I distinctly recall you saying you'd visit him and clear away any half-truths Billy and I may have inadvertently spread about you," Sally insisted, annoyed.

"Oh," Skye sighed in relief. "I guess I did say something to that effect."

"Well, are you going?"

Skye knew from past experience there would be no appeasing her friend until she conceded. It would solve everything to make a quick stop on the third floor and leave a message for Jordan saying she couldn't make it after all. At the same time she would be satisfying Sally.

"I suppose a few minutes wouldn't hurt," she said with a twinge of guilt.

A bubble of elation rose from Sally. "You're not wearing that, are you?"

Skye's gaze slid down over the cream-colored silk blouse and caramel wool suit. She hadn't changed clothes, coming directly from school to the hospital. "What's wrong with what I'm wearing?"

"Have you got a year?" Sally asked with an exasperated sigh. "You really should think about going home and changing."

"You're being ridiculous," Skye said with a bit

of disbelief. The outfit was one of her best. Although plain and practical, it suited her.

"Well, we'll just have to make the best with what we've got."

"Sally," Skye expelled the name in a long, drawn-out breath, "I look fine. I'm going exactly as I am." It was easy to read the disappointment in Sally's eyes.

"Unfasten the top buttons at least," Sally entreated.

"No." Skye shook her head but couldn't help smiling at her friend's insistence.

"Okay, but at least let your hair down. I never have understood why you insist on wearing it up when it's so pretty down."

"I very seldom wear my hair down." Skye flushed slightly, remembering she had done so yesterday. No, it would be far safer to keep her hair in its tightly coiled chignon. "Another time maybe." She smiled gently.

The large doors of the elevator glided open silently, welcoming Skye to the third floor. The nurse she'd met in Jordan's room the night before nodded in recognition.

"Hello," Skye said, and smiled. "I wonder if it would be possible to leave a message for Mr. Kiley in 324."

Dark eyes stared back at Skye blankly for a moment. "I'm sorry, dear, but Jordan Kiley was discharged this afternoon."

"Oh." Skye felt a sudden loss for words.

"It's my understanding he's returning to Los Angeles." The nurse continued, "I'm sure the hospital can relay his address if you care to contact administration."

"No, that's fine." Somehow Skye had to believe Jordan planned this deliberately. It suited his twisted sense of justice to do one up on her. A confused mixture of relief, anger and a strange disappointment overwhelmed her. "Thank you," she said, and smiled weakly at the nurse before turning back to the elevator.

By Friday evening Skye still hadn't shaken the feeling of melancholy; instead of being pensive and a little depressed, she should be grateful for the reprieve. She'd never intended to continue seeing Jordan and should be counting her blessings instead of acting disappointed.

She was mixing together a chicken salad for dinner when her doorbell rang. Sighing heavily, she abandoned the salad, wondering what John wanted to borrow this time. Did the man ever do any grocery shopping, she wondered.

She crossed the living room, wiping her hands on her apron as she went. Opening the door, the good-natured, tolerant smile froze on her face. Shock closed her mouth, but for the life of her she couldn't utter a single word.

"Hello again." Jordan smiled suavely, not in the least affected by her obvious surprise. His arm was in a cast and supported by a white linen sling, but that did little to mar his compelling features. The charcoal gray of his pants and the smoky amber sweater accentuated the clear gray of his eyes. Skye had always considered herself statuesque, but he stood four or five inches taller than she, seeming to dwarf her.

"Jordan," she whispered incredulously as the shock slowly dissipated.

"The very same," he told her mockingly. "May I come in?"

"Oh, of course." She hurriedly stepped aside and closed the door after him, leaning against it for support as he leisurely walked into her apartment.

"Can I get you something?" she asked somewhat stiffly, unable to gain her poise.

"No, I have a taxi waiting."

This seemed to relax her slightly. He certainly wouldn't be staying long with a taxi meter running.

"I'm happy to see you haven't eaten." His gaze left her flushed face momentarily, and he eyed the lettuce and chicken on her kitchen countertop. "I made the dinner reservation for eight, so you have plenty of time to change if you wish. However, what you're wearing is fine."

"Dinner?" she swallowed uncomfortably. "Oh, I couldn't. I mean . . ." Her mind searched frantically for a logical excuse to refuse. She immediately knew why he hadn't contacted her in advance. Apparently he knew her well enough to realize that given time, she would have somehow extracted herself from the date. Now she was trapped.

"I won't take no for an answer, Skye." Determination narrowed his eyes.

"All right," she agreed weakly. "Just give me a few minutes to put the food away in the kitchen." She wouldn't change clothes, not with the practical side of her nature adding the toll of the waiting cab.

She glanced at herself briefly in the hallway mirror as she reached for her earth-tone blazer. The jacket went nicely with her rust-colored oxford pleated pants.

"I'm ready." She paused, feeling gauche and insecure. "Are you sure this outfit is okay?"

His dark brows lifted, and a smile touched the corners of his hard mouth. "You might want to wear shoes."

If a hole had developed in the earth's crust, Skye would have gladly leaped inside. Her face flushed a deep shade of pink, and she nodded lamely. She had always had a ridiculous habit of walking around the apartment barefooted. It was second nature to slip off her shoes the minute she walked in the door. Luckily her heels were in the entryway, and turning her back to Jordan, she slipped them on slowly, giving her racing heart a chance to quiet. But when his hand settled on her shoulder and his husky voice sounded in her ear, she found her pulse rate anything but normal.

"The apron," he reminded her. "I'm taking you out to eat. I don't expect you to have to cook."

Her trembling fingers immediately reached behind her back to untie the knot. What was it about Jordan Kiley that turned her into a bumbling, forgetful idiot?

The restaurant was one Skye had never heard of before. The dining area was small and contained only a small number of tables. The interior was dimly lit by flickering candles upon elegantly set tables. A single long-stemmed rose set in a crystal vase served as the centerpiece.

Once they were seated and studying the menus, the waiter returned. "Would you care for something to drink?" Jordan asked.

"A drink?" Skye realized she sounded like an echo. "No . . . I don't think so . . . not now, anyway."

Jordan ordered wine, and the waiter returned with the bottle, complimenting him on his choice. It was when he was testing the wine that she noticed his right hand. He now enjoyed the freedom of his fingers, although a thin layer of gauze covered a major portion of his hand.

His gaze followed hers, and he flexed his fingers for her benefit. "The doctor changed the dressing the day I was discharged. I imagine you're relieved to know it won't be necessary for you to cut my meat."

"I wasn't worried," she smiled, beginning to relax.

"Have you decided what you'd like to order?" His menu was folded beside his plate; apparently he had made his decision already.

The menu ran the full gamut, but the prices were outrageously high, and Skye chose the least expensive item.

"I'll have the Chicken Florentine." She closed her menu, and as if on cue the waiter appeared.

"I'd like to propose a toast," Jordan suggested, tipping his wine goblet to gently tap her water glass. "To Pollyanna, whose radiant smile could melt a polar ice cap." His own smile, directed at her, left Skye feeling weak.

A few minutes later their salad was served. Skye was grateful for the diversion; the atmosphere was quickly becoming intimate.

"I ordered dessert for us," Jordan announced, his gray eyes briefly meeting hers. "I hope you have no objection to flaming baked Alaska."

"Baked Alaska." She swallowed convulsively, a smile trembling at the corner of her mouth. "I'm surprised you forgot the violinist." It was important to maintain this lighthearted banter; only when she could laugh and tease did she feel at ease.

Throwing her a sideways glance, Jordan reached

across the table and rang a small bell. Almost immediately two violinists strolled into the room.

Against her will Skye burst into helpless laughter. The palm of her hand covered her mouth to hide the outburst.

A full smile tugged at Jordan's mouth. "Is any romantic dinner complete without music?" He quirked his brow in question.

"Jordan Kiley, I don't think I've met anyone like you in my entire life," she managed, shaking her head at him. "You're hopeless." But she didn't question why he'd gone to such lengths to create a romantic atmosphere for her.

The chicken was succulent and tender, and as long as Skye concentrated on the meal the intimacy was held to a minimum.

"Do you know all of the volunteers on the children's ward?" Jordan inquired lazily as the waiter replenished his glass of wine.

"Of course; I've been a volunteer for several years," she replied.

"Who plays the piano and sings?" His dark eyes watched her closely.

Skye was mildly surprised Sally and Billy hadn't supplied him with the information but was strangely reluctant to reveal herself. She hesitated momentarily. She didn't want the evening to center around her, nor did she wish to answer the inevitable question, Why don't you turn professional?

"That's Jane." It wasn't a lie. Jane was her name; she had been dubbed Skye after a growing spurt in the sixth grade had shot her head and shoulders above every boy in class. The name had stuck and now most people knew her by her nickname.

Skye was certain Jordan wished to question her further, but she hurriedly stood, asking to be excused. The ladies' room offered a quiet moment of solitude where she could relax. She couldn't deny her attraction for Jordan but at the same time realized how pointless and dangerous the attraction was. He obviously felt he owed her a dinner and had very possibly delayed his return to L.A. to settle his debt. Now she must be gracious enough to allow him to satisfy his sense of obligation.

When she returned to his table, Jordan had ordered coffee.

"Have you ridden the cable cars yet?" she asked before he could pursue his questions.

Jordan glanced at her a bit suspiciously. "Not yet."

"You really should," Skye insisted. "You haven't truly savored San Francisco's uniqueness until you ride the cable cars."

"Oh?" Jordan's smile was mocking, and swaying his broken arm outward, he added, "I think I've had enough of a taste of San Francisco."

Skye loved her city and was undeterred by his lack of enthusiasm. "I bet you didn't know that the cable cars were invented by a horse lover."

"No, I didn't." His gaze lifted from his coffee to study her.

"It's true. A man by the name of Andrew Hallidie felt sorry for the horses who sometimes slipped on the steep hills and broke their legs. So Hallidie invented the cable car. By 1890 San Francisco had eight major systems operating within the city limits. The idea caught on elsewhere, too. I bet you didn't know that Los Angeles also used cable cars for a while."

"When was that?"

Skye realized she must sound very much like the teacher she was, but his eyes expressed interest. "Back in 1887. Now, are you ready to ride a cable car?"

"After a history lesson like that, I dare not refuse." His returning smile was full and warm and had a crazy effect upon Skye.

Friday evenings were always a busy traffic night for the cable cars, and Jordan and Skye were forced to wait a few minutes before boarding.

"Where are we headed?" Jordan asked indulgently as they stepped aboard.

"Fisherman's Wharf." Skye laughed, her smiling features profiled in the moonlight. "You really must see the Wharf before you leave."

"You've missed your calling." Jordan's eyes also smiled. "You should have been a travel guide."

The ride was exhilarating. Jordan's good arm cradled her around the waist and gripped the wooden column behind her. Skye didn't object to the intimate hold; she felt warm and secure with the strength of his arm around her.

Colorful and amusing, the cable car operator chatted loudly with his customers, calling out the street names and amusing bits of information.

"These boys seem to be a unique breed," Jordan said with a throaty chuckle, watching the gripman push and pull the long lever that connected the cable running underground, towing the car.

"We're unique all right," the cable man laughed. "They only hire people who are half crazy. You have to be looney to take a job like this one."

All too soon the invigorating ride had ended. Crowds were thick on the Wharf's wide sidewalks, even though it was well into the evening. The permeating aroma of salt water and fish drifted pleasingly to their senses. Hundreds of vessels comprising the fishing fleet were docked at the pier.

They strolled hand in hand, not speaking until Skye pointed to the boats. "Over three million pounds of fish are caught every year by our industrious fleet. Sardines account for most of that, with crabs running in a close second."

"Do you enjoy crab meat?" Jordan asked unexpectedly.

"Far more than I like sardines," she joked lightly.

Several vendors had set up shop on the sidewalks, and a lovely seashell necklace caught Skye's attention.

"Look." She stopped to examine the delicate shells. The tiny shells laid gently across the palm of her hand. "It's my niece's birthday soon. This would be perfect. Janey's just the right age to appreciate something this lovely, and she has a seashell collection."

"I'll buy it," Jordan offered immediately.

"Oh, no." She gently laid a restraining hand against his arm. "You mustn't. The gift would be from you then, not me."

"All right," he agreed reluctantly. "But one thing."

"Yes?" Her eye sought his.

"Are you going to take off your shoe?"

A corner of her mouth twitched upward as she fought to suppress a smile. "No, I think I can manage it."

They decided to stop for a cup of coffee at a small restaurant against the sea. Fish, crab and other delicacies were displayed under a bed of crushed ice outside the restaurant doors. An old seaman, a stained white apron hugging his chest and waist and black rubbers on his feet, smiled up at them before they entered.

"Good evening, folks. Enjoy your dinner. It's a night for young lovers." He looked into the clear sky. The stars shone like jewels on a blanket of black velvet.

"It is a beautiful night," Skye admitted, her face flushed with embarrassment.

"Yes, beautiful." Jordan added his agreement, but he wasn't looking into the sky.

The coffee was dark and strong. Skye was grateful for its potency. She needed to be reminded, in a down-to-earth manner, that this little excursion was a one-time experience. It would be too easy to allow herself to fall under Jordan's powerful spell. He was a rare kind of man, both confident and totally masculine, and she didn't doubt he used his charm to achieve whatever he purposed. She faked a subtle yawn.

"You're tired?"

Skye had difficulty meeting his look. "It's been a long week. . . . Maybe it would be best if I did head home."

Skye would have willingly caught the bus that would have taken her directly to her apartment, but Jordan wouldn't hear of it and insisted upon a taxi. Her heart hammered frantically when they arrived at her building, and Jordan dismissed the cab.

"You weren't going to invite me in?" He looked into her confused eyes.

"Well, actually . . . no." She spoke bluntly. "I'm not in the habit of entertaining men in my apartment late at night." She knew she sounded very prim and proper, but that couldn't be helped. His laughing eyes riled her further. "I'm glad you think it's so funny," she burst out irritably.

He ignored her outburst and took the keys from her trembling hand. "And as a proper gentleman, I consider it my duty to escort you safely to your door."

Skye was forced to follow him and did so ungraciously. The hallway outside her door was well lit and Skye offered a silent prayer of thanksgiving that her landlord had recently installed brighter light bulbs.

"I enjoyed the dinner. Thank you, Jordan," she said as soon as he had unlocked the door. She extended her hand, ready to accept her keys, her knees suddenly weak at his close proximity. The cold metal felt good against her outstretched hand as he placed the chain there and gently folded her hand closed. With his forefinger tucked beneath her chin he raised her downcast gaze to meet his. Forced to meet his eyes, Skye felt a flood of warmth sweep over her. His eyes were no longer laughing but warm and sensuous. She wanted to back away from him and break the spell, but the force of his command was so strong, she couldn't blink.

The pressure of his hand moved from her chin to the back of her neck, his fingers sliding into her hair. Slowly his mouth descended to hers. Skye could have protested, but she didn't utter a sound.

Caught in the powerful pull of her senses, her eyes closed slowly, the curiosity to discover his kiss overpowering.

His mouth was warm and gentle, the pressure light and sweet, as if he understood her need for tenderness. Fighting the clamoring of her nerves that had suddenly burst into life, Skye remained frozen, unable to respond and equally unable to break away.

When the pressure of the kiss ended, Skye remained caught in the sensations, her eyes shut. Only when Jordan's hand pulled away from her hair did she find the strength to look at him. Moving aside, he turned the knob of her door and pushed it open for her.

"Good night, Skye," he whispered huskily.

She stared at him blankly for a moment.

"Don't look at me like that," he groaned. "Now, go inside before I change my mind."

His threat, indeed promise, quickly broke the spell, and Skye hurried inside, welcoming the safety of home.

Chapter Four

Saturday morning the skies were overcast, leaden gray clouds gloomily forecasting a day only a true San Franciscan could love.

Skye woke in good spirits; she had enjoyed herself last night. Unwillingly she admitted that Jordan was good company, but made no attempt to analyze her feelings regarding his kiss. It had been her moment of reckoning; she owed him the kiss. As for his surprise visit and the dinner, it had just been his way of settling a debt. She had bought the pizza, and his pride demanded recompense. He was probably on his way back to Los Angeles by now, and she could close the door on this short episode, remembering him fondly.

The Saturday morning housework took almost two hours and with the last load of washing folded, Skye sat down with a good book. The latest study on child behavior she had purchased had come highly recommended, and she had been looking forward to reading it.

Yet hardly a word filtered through her thoughts. Somehow the picture of the violinists strolling into the restaurant kept flitting through her mind. Skye couldn't refrain from laughing all over again. No wonder Jordan had looked so pleased when she had teasingly said all they needed were violinists. She had fallen right into his trap.

The old seaman had thought they were lovers. Jordan Kiley probably had lots of lovers; he was definitely a man of the world. She wondered why he had never married, but suddenly realized that for all she knew he could have a wife conveniently tucked away. Somehow the idea wasn't feasible. No, he was too straightforward and candid to cheat on a wife. She didn't doubt he was an experienced lover, but believed that for all his experience he didn't know love as God intended it to be. Jordan Kiley was like so many others, seeking to fill a void in his life that could only be satisfied by Christ.

Reading was useless; setting aside the book, Skye changed into her jogging clothes. It looked like rain, but that didn't bother her. She often jogged in the rain; the cool drops splashing against her face were refreshing and invigorating.

She followed her usual route, running around the green at the Marina. The sultry breeze rolling in from the Pacific teased her. It seemed to be whispering Jordan's name. As if to free herself she tossed her head back. Her long hair, driven from her face, flowed gracefully behind her. Yet the action did little to dispel Jordan's presence from her mind. If she listened carefully, she could almost hear his husky voice calling her.

"This is silly," she said aloud. To allow this one unnerving man to throw her now was like succumbing to a temporary kind of madness. She had long before accepted God's plan for her life and didn't regret being single.

As if to outrun her thoughts, Skye jogged twice as far as normal and was exhausted by the time she stopped to walk the remaining blocks home. Walking home gave her body a chance to cool down after the long run and was as vital as the warm-up exercises she ritually performed before running. Yet she didn't feel herself cooling down. It was as if her body and her mind were working against her in a fever pitch. Memories of Glen bobbed to the surface of her mind, happy ones that she'd long ago locked away. Had the short time she'd been with Jordan done this to her? From past experience she realized she needed to keep herself busy, push the memories away.

After a short shower Skye changed clothes and left almost immediately, although she had no real destination in mind.

"Anyone home?" Skye knocked loudly on the varnished door before letting herself in.

"Skye?" Peggy Garvin came from the kitchen, a large terrycloth apron tied around her slim waist. Bursting with the news of her pregnancy, Peggy threw her arms around her sister-in-law.

"Brad told you, didn't he?" she said, hugging Skye close.

"Of course. He never could keep a secret for long," Skye said, returning the affectionate hug. She stepped back and carefully studied the happiness in Peggy's eyes. "You show already."

Peggy's hand automatically rested against her flat stomach as her gaze swept downward. "Do you really think so?" she asked.

"Not there, silly," Skye chided. "It's that radiant gleam."

"I know, I know. I don't think I've been more pleased about anything in my life. What are we doing standing here? Let's go into the kitchen. I'm baking cookies. Chocolate chip—your favorite."

"These smell good. Mind if I help myself?" She didn't bother to wait for permission but bit into the melting morsel, savoring the chocolate flavor.

Peggy pulled another sheet from the oven and carefully lifted the cookies with her spatula onto a waiting rack. "This is the last of the batch. Let's have some tea; I picked up a new flavor at the store the other day. How does cherry almond sound?" Stretching her petite frame to reach the top cupboard, Peggy brought down her best china cups. "Only the best for us," she declared.

The spicy aroma of the tea pervaded the room as they chatted.

"It's so good to see you, Skye. How have you been?"

"I should be asking you that question. How are you feeling?" Although her attention was directed on Peggy, her fingers were making lazy circles around the rim of her teacup. "You're taking good care of yourself, aren't you?"

"Heavens, yes! Oh, Skye, the Lord is so good. I'm still having trouble believing I'm really pregnant, after all these years." Some of the enthusiasm left Peggy's eyes. "Now, if only Brad could find a job."

"Speaking of my dear brother, where is he?"

"He told me he was going to help a friend move, but I know differently." Peggy shifted uneasily. "He's out again looking for a job, any job. With a baby on the way Brad feels such a sense of urgency." Her fingers tugged nervously on her bottom lip. "I guess I do too. My moods swing from elation and ecstasy to doubt and worry."

Skye had the same feelings herself. Although very pleased for her brother and his family, she couldn't chase away a feeling of unease. She realized her family was in God's hands, but reminding Peggy of this sounded trite and overused.

"Do you remember the Joyce Landorf series we saw at church last year?" asked Skye.

Peggy nodded.

"I guess this is what she meant by being stuck in a waiting room."

"Yes, with both exits covered."

It was Skye's turn to smile. "You know, I'd do anything in the world to help you."

"We know, Skye, and thanks, but Brad's pride is at stake now. You've done too much already."

Skye studied her sister-in-law seriously. "Don't let pride get in your way, Peg."

She paused, searching Skye's face. "You've met someone, haven't you?"

Taken back by Peggy's directness, Skye flushed slightly and lowered her gaze. "What makes you say that?" she said, trying hard to hide any telltale inflection of surprise in her voice.

"You look, well . . ." Again Peggy hesitated, as if searching for the right word. "Happier . . . brighter, as if some spark has been ignited again. Brad mentioned something too. He said you'd obviously been dating someone because you closed up like a clam the minute he asked about it."

"I guess you could say I've met someone," Skye admitted reluctantly.

"And?" Peggy probed.

"It's someone from the hospital. He was in a car accident and has a broken arm. It was in traction for a while, but he's been discharged now."

Peggy's eyes rounded at the information and twinkled with delight.

"It's no big deal, Peggy. Honest," Skye stressed. "I enjoyed his company, but it's not what you think. He's from L.A. and has returned home."

"Is he handsome?"

Skye tilted her head thoughtfully and shrugged noncommittally. "I'd say he was, but not strikingly so." Unconsciously she stiffened; this was dangerous territory. Her own feelings for Jordan were a mystery. How could she explain them to another?

Peggy seemed to understand her indecision and

smiled in return. "Any time you show this much interest in a man, I can't help getting excited. I don't mean to pry, but honestly, Skye, Glen's been gone a long time. Too many years for you to continue on the way you have been."

A guarded expression came over Skye's face. Glen's name was rarely mentioned. Brad and Peggy had always been sensitive to her grief. "What are you saying?" she asked brusquely.

Peggy sighed, almost as if she were unwilling to continue. "You've been living your life in a shell. For eight years there hasn't been anything or anyone who has been able to bring you back to reality, and it's time you realized that."

It was unlike Peggy to be so blunt or hurtful. "That's not true," Skye said defensively, the tiny hairs on the back of her neck bristling. "Glen and I shared something unique. Our life together would have been very special, but for you to insist I've built a wall around myself is totally false." She paused, gathering the strength of conviction. "I have to think very hard to clearly remember what Glen even looked like."

Peggy was watching Skye with concern. "We seem to have gotten off the track, haven't we?"

Swallowing determinedly at the tight lump in her throat, Skye gave a wavering smile. "We certainly have. I came to congratulate you and discuss Janey's birthday present. How would you and Brad feel if I got her a puppy?"

"A puppy?" Peggy echoed, sounding aghast.

"Sally's dog recently had a litter, and she's offered me first choice. You remember Sally, my friend from St. John's."

"Of course." Peggy's eyebrows arched thoughtfully. "You know it might not be a bad idea. With the baby coming it could be just the thing for Janey. I'll talk to Brad."

The remainder of the visit was strained, with both women pretending an ease neither felt. Skye left shortly afterward.

Confused and unsettled, Skye drove home in a thoughtful mood. How could Peggy have said such hurtful things? She had worked hard to overcome her grief. It was true that for a while she had lost her will to live. Something deep within her had died with Glen. But she was a free spirit now, free to love and be loved. Hadn't she always been? Peggy had never hurt her this way before. It was true she seldom dated anyone for long, but that wasn't because she was carrying a torch for Glen. There were very few men who interested her. Certainly all the dates Sally had arranged over the years should prove something to Peggy. Nonetheless her sister-in-law's attitude hurt.

About a mile from home the car coughed and sputtered. Skye tensed. "Not again," she groaned inwardly. Suddenly the buzzer to her seat belt began to hiss, although it was connected. The radio began making eerie, high-pitched screeches, fading in and out. She had purposely turned it off in order to think. Quickly she pulled her small Ford to the curb before it gave one final cough and died.

"Blast it." Her hand banged the steering wheel impatiently. Anger and outrage began churning. She tried turning the ignition key but was met with silence.

"I can't believe it!" She jerked open her car door, got out and slammed it angrily. She didn't even bother to look under the hood, knowing it was useless.

It began to rain about halfway home, an angry torrent that added fuel to her bad mood. She was drenched by the time she arrived at her apartment building. Heavy drops of rain ran off her hair and face as she paused to unlock her door.

John Dirkson stuck his head out of his apartment. "Hello, Sweet Stuff." He greeted her with a flashy grin. "I see you got yourself all wet and cold. I'm perfectly willing to warm you up," he offered, with all the subtlety of a garden serpent.

"Oh, shut up, John," Skye stormed, and slammed her door in his surprised face.

No more than two minutes later her doorbell rang impatiently.

Stamping her foot irritably, she turned off the bath water. Luckily she hadn't gotten around to undressing.

"Don't hassle me, John, I'm in no mood to—"

She stopped dead in midsentence. It was Jordan. What was he doing here? Oh, God, why hadn't he returned to L.A.? Why didn't he just get out of her life?

"Do I detect a note of anger?" he asked, amused, letting himself in.

Skye gave a short sarcastic laugh. "Angry? Me? That's my problem: I don't have the common sense to get good and mad every now and then. People think they can take advantage of me, that I won't fight back. They think of me as Holly Holiness."

Irrationally she paced the floor, waving her hands.

"A Pollyanna?" Jordan inserted.

"Exactly!" She stopped and looked at him momentarily. "I'm as even tempered and cool-headed as the next person. But I'll only be driven so far."

The amusement left Jordan's eyes. "What's wrong?"

"You know what my problem is?" She didn't wait for his answer. "I never let loose. I let people walk all over me. Well, I'm good and loose now. It's my own fault," she continued, pacing. "I don't smoke. I don't swear. I've never marched in a protest rally. I didn't even burn my bra when it was the popular thing to do." She stopped to take a quick breath. "Well, I've had just about as much as I'm going to take."

"Skye?"

She ignored him.

"Skye?" he spoke louder.

"I'm taking the mechanic to court. I'll sue him for every penny. He'll . . ."

She didn't get the opportunity to finish. Jordan swiftly jerked her arm around, pulling her against him. Before she could protest, his mouth captured hers.

Taken completely by surprise, Skye felt the anger drain away, replaced by a budding awareness. She was frightened that she should respond to him like this, all consideration of her anger and her plight erased by a single action.

She broke the contact, raising her questioning eyes to his. His look trapped her, warm and sensual. Slowly his hand slid over her back, drawing her to him.

Taking an uneven breath in confusion, Skye made a feeble attempt to break away. Undaunted, he continued the gentle caress, slowly drawing her into his protective hold. When he lowered his mouth to hers, her lips parted in anticipation.

Why does it have to be him, her mind questioned unreasonably. His very touch seemed to bring her suddenly back to life. She was caught in the sensual awareness and yet felt frightened and unsure. If this continued, Jordan Kiley could easily become a weakness she might not be able to overcome. Forcefully she tore her lips from his, and taking a deep breath, she struggled to regain her bearings.

"Jordan, please, this is important," she insisted.

"I know," he said, his voice thick and husky as he explored the side of her neck.

"Please, stop." She was breathless yet fervent. "Kissing me isn't going to fix my car."

He straightened, his mouth curving into smiling grooves. "Ah, but my arm aches considerably less."

She broke contact, moving purposefully away from him. "I . . . I think aspirin would work far more effectively."

He shrugged, his glance focusing on her lips as if to say it wasn't aspirin he was interested in.

Her pique rose. "Darn it, Jordan Kiley, don't look at me like that. I'm stuck with a useless piece of junk, and you want to play spin the bottle."

Promptly he pulled her back into his arms and placed a quick kiss upon her unsuspecting lips. "Settle down, or I'll be forced to take drastic measures."

She stared up at him wordlessly, swallowing tightly.

"Now, what's wrong with your car?"

She couldn't answer. Her heart was hammering so wildly it made clear thinking impossible. She lowered her head, not wanting Jordan to see the effect he had on her.

His free hand gently lifted her face. "Your car?"

"It's not running again." Her voice didn't sound right, even to herself. "It stalled last week, and I couldn't get it started. I phoned the car dealership where I'd bought it, and they put a new battery in. The mechanic said since the car is three years old, that probably was the problem."

"Who's the mechanic?"

"George somebody. He works for Olsen Ford, where I bought the car."

"And?"

"Well, it died again the other day, and this George said it needed a new alteration."

"Alternator," Jordan supplied with a grin.

"Whatever!" she said irritably. "Anyway, the car did it again today. That's why I'm drenched. I had to leave it and walk home."

A flickering light of anger entered his eyes. "I'll handle it for you."

"No," she challenged sharply. "It's going to give me a great deal of pleasure to talk to these people."

A light rap on her door stiffened her instinctively. She wasn't expecting anyone.

A tall, well-dressed man of towering bulk greeted her.

"Jordan here?" He placed heavy emphasis on *Jordan,* his expression alive with amusement.

"Bill." The name was issued with no welcome as Jordan moved toward the man. "I said I'd only be a minute."

The huge man shrugged his shoulders. "I got tired of waiting," was the only excuse he offered. "Aren't you going to introduce me?"

"Bill Malloy, Skye Garvin." The introduction was issued grudgingly.

Bill Malloy smiled warmly at Skye and his strong hand closed firmly over hers. "You're everything Jordan said and more." He released her hand slowly. His eyes, trapping hers, possessed a mocking gleam.

"Weren't we on our way to a meeting?" Jordan asked curtly.

"We were." Bill smiled. "I know how Dan hates to be kept waiting."

"Then let's get moving." Jordan's voice sounded thin and brittle.

"It was a pleasure meeting you, Skye." His eyes continued to hold hers.

"Yes," she said in some confusion. Her attention darted from one man to the other. Bill was finding something highly amusing, but what? Jordan was recognizably upset. His lips were firmly compressed, as if he were holding his anger tightly in check.

"I'll phone you," he promised Skye, ushering his friend out the door. Gently his hand touched her cheek.

Skye watched them go, thoroughly bewildered. Jordan had never mentioned why he'd stopped by. Although he hadn't said he was returning to L.A.,

Skye had received the impression he was. She honestly hadn't expected to see him again.

A shiver danced over her skin, reminding her she was wet. She didn't care to ponder the question of what exactly had caused her skin to quiver.

The bath water steamed up the bathroom mirror. It was a luxury to linger in the tub. Skye could actually feel the hot water chase away her chill. Spooning the moisture over herself with the washcloth, her thoughts drifted back to her visit with Peggy. It was almost unbelievable that her sister-in-law would talk to her like that. And because the things Peggy said were so untrue, it hurt all the more. Skye had come so far, considering that the grief had been overwhelming at first. It was as if the pieces of her life had crumbled before her. But simply because she was a living, breathing soul, she found herself forced into a resilient, elastic world. Although others cared, they couldn't know the emotional torture she had endured. Suddenly a gnawing pain swelled inside her until her eyes burned with tears.

Resting her head against the back of the tub, she stared sightlessly at the ceiling, tears streaming unheeded down her face. Could it be that Peggy was right? Had all this grief lain just below the surface, not really being dealt with at all? Skye examined the last eight years of her life. Had she really made a martyr of herself? Deflecting male relationships and commitment to another man? But Glen had been so special. He was the only man she'd ever loved, ever wanted. Loving another would betray what they had shared. It had been cruel and heartless to take him from her.

It came to her then. Profound and deep. The shock raised goose bumps over her pale skin, although she lay in a tub of steaming water. *She blamed God for taking Glen.* Over the years she had yielded other areas of her life to her Lord but had stubbornly withheld this one facet of her Christian walk. Her faith had been smaller than a mustard seed. Instead of looking upon his death and all that followed as having worked together for her good, Skye had never forgiven God.

Rising from her bath, she wrapped a towel around herself and faced the bathroom mirror. With jerking movements she wiped away the steam to examine herself. Sally was right; her hairstyle—the coiled bun—was harsh and purposely unattractive. With troubled eyes and her heart hammering, she pulled the pins and watched her hair tumble down. It needed to be cut to a more manageable length. Her pale cheeks looked bloodless and waxen. How long had it been since she'd purposely made herself attractive? But perhaps she looked wan because she was seeing herself with new soul-searching eyes.

She dressed quickly, an urgency driving her.

Throwing open the doors to her closet, she critically examined its contents. Her clothes were outdated and unappealing—beiges, grays, browns and blacks. The exceptions were a few colorful outfits her family had given her for Christmas and her birthday.

Perhaps most profound was how she'd maintained her wit and sense of humor. Her natural good taste in clothes and style had wavered dramatically over the years, but not her enthusiasm and vitality. Instinctively she knew if she'd allowed this bizarre grief to infiltrate the core of her personality, she would have shriveled up and died in a unique form of suicide.

"Oh, Father," her soul cried out, "forgive me, forgive me." She fell to her knees beside the bed and buried her face in her hands. A peaceful silence filled the room as she surrendered this part of her life to her Lord. Time lost meaning as Skye poured out her heart, and when she rose she felt as if a heavy burden had been lifted from her, an eight-year-old yoke she had bound to herself. She was free to love and be loved . . . at last.

Later that evening she idly flipped through the pages of the *TV Guide*, a smile played at the corner of her lips. She felt like a new woman and stood to examine herself again. . . . A smiling stranger was reflected back. She had spent most of the afternoon on a one-woman crusade to create a new image for herself, and she was pleased with the results.

Her first concern had been her car. She called the dealership expecting to do battle, but the mechanic stumbled all over himself apologizing. He didn't know what the problem was, but he would look into it immediately. He worked so quickly, Skye was stunned. He stopped at her house for her keys; had her car towed to the shop and returned, all within forty-five minutes. It had been a cut wire, he explained with chagrin. There was no charge.

Her first stop had been at the beautician's, who'd cut only an inch or two from the length of her hair. An overall treatment added body and vitality to the silky gold strands.

Now it curled beautifully around her shoulders like a gilded wreath highlighted by beams of moonlight. In her closet hung three new outfits in attractive colors. The old clothes were packed away in sacks, ready to be donated to charity. A warm smile quivered at the corner of her mouth as she remembered Sally's reaction that afternoon.

"Skye?" Sally had asked in a questioning tone, almost as if she didn't recognize her friend. "I like it, I like it." Enthusiastically she circled Skye, nodding her head approvingly. "Holy mackerel, what happened to you?" Sally laughed gaily. "No, there's no need to answer that, I already know. . . . Jordan Kiley happened to you. I knew it was coming someday, I just never thought I'd live to see it." She clapped her hands with the enthusiasm of a young child.

"Come on, you're embarrassing me." Skye grinned. "But *no*—" she waved her hand to press her point "—it's not Jordan Kiley." It was only a partial lie. The transformation had come as a result of her talk with Peggy.

"Oh?" Sally sounded skeptical. "Is there someone else I don't know about?"

"Have you met John Dirkson, my neighbor?" Skye asked coyly, instantly regretting the implication.

"You know darn good and well I haven't." Sally wrinkled her nose in suspicion. "Tell me about him."

This was becoming more than a half truth, and Skye lowered her head guiltily, hoping to hide her discomfort by picking up one of the puppies chewing at the toe of her shoe. "There isn't much to tell." She prayed for a nonchalant, devil-may-care attitude. "The reason I stopped by is to tell you I would be taking one of the puppies. It's Janey's birthday soon, and I thought this fluffy little rascal would make an excellent gift."

"My dear friend, you know the path leading directly to my heart," Sally noted dramatically. "Are you certain you wouldn't care for the other one as well? It would be a shame to separate them. Besides, if you took both of these well-behaved, royal-blooded mutts, all my problems would be solved."

"Dreamer," Skye said pointedly, and laughed as Sally hung her head in despair.

Several hours later, the apartment felt lonely and lifeless. Loud rock music blared from the wild party across the hall. Involuntarily Skye tapped her foot to the beat of the slower ballads, which blared in equal volume. For the first time in years her feet yearned to dance. Unbidden, the image of dancing with Jordan rose to her mind, and she bit her lip at the appeal the image conjured.

When the phone suddenly began ringing, Skye jerked around, caught off guard by the unexpectedness.

Two rings.

It had to be Jordan. He'd said he was going to phone, and he was a man of his word.

Three rings.

She stared mutely at the ringing phone, frozen to her chair.

Four rings.

She had made such a fool of herself this afternoon.

Five rings.

How could she have ranted and raved like that?

Six rings.

How could she have said those things?

Silence.

Skye breathed again.

Chapter Five

Hauling her guitar, Bible and purse from the parking lot to the church, Skye found Peggy waiting for her in the foyer.

"Skye," Peggy said, looking troubled and uncertain, "I like your hair. When did you have it cut?" she asked haltingly.

"Yesterday afternoon. . . . And thanks, I like it too." She accepted the compliment but wondered how long it would take Peggy to notice the real change.

Tears shimmered in Peggy's eyes. "I want to apologize for yesterday. I was blunt and rude. Will you forgive me?" It was apparent from her hurried speech that their conversation had weighed heavily on her mind.

Tears misted Skye's deep blue eyes. "Of course I will, Peg. But there's no need to apologize. Most of what you said was true."

"Perhaps, but there were nicer ways of saying it." Her fingers wiped away the moisture from her cheek, and she gave a half laugh. "We better get to class before we turn into Water Works, Incorporated, right here in the church foyer."

Skye laughed too, touched by the thoughtfulness of her sister-in-law. "I'll talk to you later." Impulsively she set her guitar down and gave

Peggy an affectionate hug before making her way to the Youth Department downstairs.

Working with the youth. Sunday mornings offered Skye a challenge completely different from her kindergarteners. One Skye enjoyed. She was the Sunday School teacher for the eighth grade group and was also in charge of the opening Sunday services.

She was met in the large meeting room by several enthusiastic hoots and a couple of wolf whistles. The youths had always been known for their liveliness, and Skye responded with a ready laugh.

The songs she led were some of the standard ones the teens enjoyed. She wandered around the room, her fingers moving agilely over the guitar strings. She paused, seeing two of the younger teen girls passing notes. Past experience had taught her that if she brought pressure from within their own peer group, any behavior problems cleared up quickly.

She stopped the song. "All right, girls." She didn't mention names but pointedly fixed her gaze on the offending class members. "This isn't the *Woody Woodpecker Hour*."

The whole class burst into laughter.

"Yeah, girls, shape up," one boy shouted, and several girls responded by sticking out their tongues.

Skye resumed the song before things got out of

hand, and soon everyone was singing again. But there was no more note passing.

Skye left church feeling elated and cheerful. The pastor's sermon had reinforced the insights revealed the day before, and she was amazed at how persistent her blindness had been.

The aroma of slowly cooking meat and vegetables met her as she entered her apartment. Skye usually ate her main meal at lunchtime on Sundays, a tradition her family had followed. Sundays were centered around the morning and evening worship services, and it was convenient to eat the main meal of the day at lunchtime.

Skye had lingered over the morning paper and was changing her clothes when the phone rang.

"Hello," she said cheerfully, expecting Peggy.

"Good afternoon," Jordan responded.

Instantly her heartbeat accelerated. She needed to explain yesterday's outburst, and it wasn't going to come easy. She so seldom lost her temper like that.

"Hello, Jordan." She hardly knew where to start. "I'm glad you phoned. . . . I feel I owe you an apology."

"Good." His crisp voice seemed to mock her. "I'll take you to lunch, and you can tell me all about it. I'll be there in twenty minutes."

The connection was broken, and Skye was left listening to the hum of the dial tone. Placing the receiver back into its cradle, Skye shrugged her shoulders. He hadn't even asked her. Jordan Kiley could be the most infuriating man. What if she had already made plans for the afternoon? She often did with her niece, Janey. Apparently any arrangements she'd made were of no consequence. She wasn't angry, but bemused. Jordan's personality was commanding and forceful, as if he were accustomed to giving orders and being obeyed. What an enigmatic man he was.

The doorbell rang well within the allotted twenty minutes. His smile was warm and lazy when she opened the door.

"Are you ready?"

"Ready?" Her round, blue eyes feigned ignorance.

"I thought we were going out to eat." Her gaze narrowed on her face.

"I don't remember your asking," she said matter-of-factly.

Catching a glimpse of the table set for two in her tiny kitchenette, Jordan expelled an angry breath. "You're expecting someone." Again it wasn't a question but a statement of fact.

"Yes, I am. You."

His gaze swiveled back to her, his thick brows knit in confusion.

"If you'd have asked me, Jordan, I'd have told you I had a meal ready in the crockpot. You're welcome to join me if you like."

He seemed to relax. Had the suspicion she was expecting someone else bothered him? The pleasure this bit of evidence brought overrode any sense of outrage at his presumptuous behavior.

His free hand gently caressed the soft flesh of her upper arm before he placed a tender kiss on her forehead.

"I'll be right back. I have a cab waiting."

Skye watched him leave. What was it about his touch that brought her senses to life? A kiss, the feather-light stroke of his hand, gave her undeniable pleasure.

Steaming bowls of Irish stew had been placed on the table by the time he returned. The smell of fresh sourdough bread filled the apartment as she drew it from the oven.

"Lunch is ready," she said, feeling awkward.

Once they were seated, Jordan paused, waiting for Skye to begin eating.

"Do you mind if we pray?" she asked unsteadily.

He arched his brows expressively. "I suspect you want more than the prayer my father taught me." His eyes were smiling. "You know the one: *Good bread, good meat, good God, let's eat.*"

Skye couldn't help laughing. "Yes, I guess I do."

"You do the honors then."

Skye bowed her head, her hands folded. "Father, thank you for abundantly supplying our needs. I would ask that you bless Jordan and our time together. Amen."

When she lifted her head, she discovered Jordan was watching her intently, and shifted uncomfortably under his scrutiny.

"Before I eat," she began haltingly, "I think I'd feel a whole lot better if I could explain about yesterday."

The smiling sparkle returned to his smoky gray eyes. "Bothers you, does it?"

She lowered her gaze, pretending to study the thick bowl of stew. "The car breaking down was a culmination of several other things. I'd had a rather disconcerting conversation with my sister-in-law, and I got caught in that cloud burst . . . and, well, I feel I owe you an apology. I don't often blow up like that, and . . ."

He reached across the small table and gently squeezed her trembling hand. "It's forgotten. Feel better?"

She smiled and nodded.

"I have to admit, however, the thought of you burning your bra is an appealing one."

Skye could feel the color invade her face, burning her cheeks. "A gentleman would have forgotten I said that."

"I'm no gentleman." His mouth quirked with the effort to suppress a laugh.

"I noticed." Determinedly Skye began eating, refusing to let him see how he had embarrassed her.

"Did you enjoy yourself last night?"

Skye didn't understand the question, and glanced at him quizzically.

"Did you and your date have a good time last night?" It was a polite inquiry without a hint of jealousy or resentment. So much for the warm satisfaction she had felt before. He really didn't care if she was with someone else or not.

"I tried phoning. You were out."

Darn, she'd forgotten his phone call. "Oh, last night. . . ." Her mind worked furiously. "Yes . . . yes, I did. I was invited to a party." Another half-truth. John Dirkson had invited her, but Skye had never considered attending. She hadn't stepped out of her apartment all evening.

They played three games of backgammon after their meal. Jordan won the first two and showed no mercy. Skye won the third because she was tired of being Ms. Nice Guy and suffered no qualms about putting him off the board. She half expected Jordan to be angry, but when she replaced his man for the third time, she saw a glimmer of respect enter his eyes.

Afterward they sat talking while they drank several cups of coffee. They found their tastes were surprisingly similar in several areas. It was when they were discussing music that he questioned her about the hospital singer for the second time.

"What's her name again," he asked with undisguised interest.

"Jane." A lump knotted her stomach.

"She's a talented lady."

"So she's been told." This was the very reason Skye didn't want him to know it was she. It embarrassed her to discuss her gift. And that was exactly what it was—a gift. She had done nothing to earn it and had always been ill-at-ease accepting compliments.

"Oh, dear, look at the time." She stood abruptly. "It's six already. I've got to be at church soon." But she had plenty of time; the evening service didn't start until six-thirty.

"Church again?" He sounded as if he didn't believe her.

"Yes, would you like to come? I'd be pleased to have you meet our pastor. I know you'll like him. My brother and his family will be there too."

Jordan stood and returned his coffee cup to the kitchen. "Another time perhaps."

She wasn't disappointed. Skye was playing the piano for the service tonight, and he was sure to guess she was the hospital singer if he saw her play.

Walking with Jordan to the small entryway, Skye could feel the muscles of her stomach begin to twitch. Was he going to try and kiss her again? Should she pretend she didn't want him to?

"Yes, I'm going to kiss you." He openly mocked her.

Her startled blue eyes flew open, and he gently

gripped her arm, bringing her to his side. "You're very easy to read sometimes." The pressure of his grip moved from her arm to the back of her neck, slowly raising her head, decreasing the distance between their lips.

Was she that transparent? Skye wondered seconds before his mouth easily fit over hers. The urgency of his kiss parted her lips, and she succumbed to the tide of sweetness that swept through her.

Embracing was awkward: The unyielding cast of his broken arm pressed painfully against her ribs as his free hand moved down the curve of her spine. But the only sensation her mind registered was the rightness of being in his arms.

"While you're in church say a prayer for me," Jordan said thickly, his voice slightly ragged.

Her voice wasn't any steadier. "I will."

The hand positioning her against him relaxed, as if he realized it must be uncomfortable for her. Skye shook her head but lowered her gaze, struggling against the magnetic pull of his eyes.

"What time does school let out these days? Maybe we can go sailing tomorrow afternoon."

"There's no school . . . it's spring break. Oh, Jordan, I can't." Regret filled her voice. "I promised Billy I was coming. Sally is making arrangements for me to take him outside the hospital for the day. I couldn't disappoint him."

"I wouldn't want you to. How about Tuesday?"

"I'd like that." She didn't even attempt to disguise her enthusiasm.

"I'll pick you up at ten."

Halfway out the door, Skye called to him. "Jordan."

He stopped and turned around.

"I *am* going to pray for you."

Something unreadable flickered from his eyes. "Do that," he said softly, and left.

On impulse Skye drove by and picked up her niece before stopping at the hospital for Billy. The two had met several times previously and seemed to enjoy one another.

"Hi ya, Sprout."

Billy was in his wheelchair waiting. "Hi, Skye; hi, Janey." His eyes lit up eagerly.

"Okay, you two, we have the whole day ahead of us. Where would you like to go?"

"Chinatown," they shouted in unison.

"Chinatown," she moaned, as if it were some great tragedy, but a laugh lay barely beneath the surface. San Francisco's Chinatown was exotic and exciting. The largest community of Chinese people living together outside the Orient, it seemed like a foreign country.

Skye located a parking place within easy access to the well-defined area and soon the three were making their way down the crowded streets. Several shops displayed signs in English, but the only language that drifted toward them was a rapid flow of Chinese.

Billy insisted upon handling the wheelchair himself, but Skye found it necessary to help him several times as they moved down the narrow, hilly streets on and off Grant Avenue. Many stores had sidewalk displays, and Billy was able to investigate the treasures of the East without having to maneuver his wheelchair through the narrow shop doors.

They stopped to eat lunch in a nearby restaurant. Ushered into a cubicle by the waiter, they were given their own private dining room. Both children loved the privacy and took delight in teasing one another, especially over the chopsticks.

The food was delicious. Janey and Billy quickly devoured the traditional Chinese dishes, leaving Skye to sample the more exotic ones. The fortune cookies were the highlight of the meal as far as either child was concerned.

"Read yours, Aunt Skye," Janey coaxed.

"You first." Skye leaned forward, feigning acute interest.

Janey cracked hers open and was immediately consumed by giggles. Billy read it for her in a sing-songy rhyme that could barely be understood above Janey's laughter. But Billy showed little interest in his and laid it beside his plate, his eyes dull and tired, yet smiling.

"What's yours say, Skye?" he wanted to know.

To appease them both she examined the tiny slip. The words seemed to reach out and slap her. BEWARE OF THE STRANGER DARK AND BOLD. STAY TRUE TO YOUR LOVE OF LONG AGO.

"It says—" she faltered slightly, "—it's time to take Billy back to the hospital."

They both objected, but not strenuously. Billy fell asleep in the car, and Janey was unusually quiet. Whether it was because she was exhausted too or as a thoughtful gesture so as not to wake Billy, Skye didn't question.

As the silence settled over the car the message of the fortune cookie kept repeating itself in her confused brain. It was uncanny, inexplicable, and the words deeply troubled her. Was God using this to warn her about Jordan? The words echoed through her mind a hundred times as she drove from the hospital to her brother's house. Although she'd made the proper responses when spoken to at the hospital, her mind was far from the matters at hand. It was something she couldn't explain or reason away. Above all else, Skye realized that nothing in her life happened by accident. God had a purpose in everything, no matter how minute.

Home looked good; her feet hurt after the extended hike. After hanging her poplin jacket in the entryway closet, she went directly to the Bible set on the nightstand. For all her years of Bible study and all the verses she'd memorized over the years, she didn't know what to make of the message of the fortune cookie.

"Dear Jesus," she began silently, sitting cross-legged across the top of her bed. "I don't know why You allowed this message to come to me, or if it has any significance at all. I realize You guide me through life and I am trusting You. Thank you, Lord, for sending Jordan into my life. At first he frightened me, and I didn't know how to handle the feeling he awoke within me. Although I find myself still unsure, I'm far less afraid. I'm asking You, Lord, to guide me in this relationship. I desire only Your will in my life."

Familiar with several books in the Bible, Skye read until she felt a soothing peace come over her spirit.

Because the situation was in God's hands, Skye forgot it, later fixing herself a light dinner. While she was washing the dishes her phone rang.

"Hello, Pollyanna. Been saying your prayers like a good girl?"

"Hello, Jordan." It was so good to talk to him, she didn't take exception to his greeting. "And, yes, I have been saying my prayers, including a few for you."

"I'm going to need them. Listen, Blue Eyes, I've got to cancel tomorrow. Things have gotten out of hand here in L.A. without me. I flew back this afternoon."

"Oh." Her heart plummeted. Jordan had left.

"That's all right," she lied. Nervously her fingers looped a strand of ashen hair around her ear.

"It's not all right," Jordan said impatiently.

The doorbell rang, jerking her attention to the apartment door. "Jordan, there's someone at my door. Hold on . . . or do you want to hang up?"

"No, I don't want to hang up. Answer the door," he said, and sighed heavily in irritation.

Laying the phone on the small table beside her davenport, Skye rushed to answer the repeated buzz. If it was John Dirkson, she thought, she'd scream.

She didn't, of course. "Yes?" she said brusquely, hoping she sounded as unfriendly as she felt.

Indolently John placed himself between Skye and the door. "Hi, Sweet Stuff. I wonder if you happen to have a tube of anchovy paste?"

"Anchovy paste?" Skye laughed. "No, John, I don't normally keep anchovy paste lying around."

"Maybe you should look," he persisted. "One never knows what lurks in the backs of cupboards."

"Listen," she said pointedly, glancing back into her living room, "I'm on the phone. It's long distance."

John beamed her one of the irresistible smiles meant to melt the defenses of the most determined woman. "I don't mind waiting." Before she could stop him, he had let himself in, sunk down on the davenport and made himself at home.

Skye sighed in frustration. "Jordan," she began self-consciously, "it's my neighbor."

"So I heard," Jordan said in a voice that sounded very much like a snarl. "I want to talk to you, Skye. Get rid of him."

Skye turned her back to John and cupped her hand over the mouth of the receiver. "I tried," she whispered spiritedly. Jordan was angry, Skye could feel his impatience. "I want to talk to you, too," she added so there would be no doubt where her preference lay.

His breath was expelled harshly. "All right, I'll phone back in ten minutes. Will that give you enough time?"

"Yes . . . yes, I think so."

Actually it took her only five minutes and a few choice words to show John exactly what she thought of his rude, insensitive behavior. Because of his unfailing belief in his male charm, Skye's repeated rejection had fueled a challenge too blatant to be ignored. When she told him that if he bothered her again she would contact the apartment manager, John looked totally confused. Women didn't usually treat his attention lightly.

The phone only rang once. "Jordan?"

He didn't bother with a greeting. "Is he gone?"

"Yes, he's gone." She took the phone and curled up on the davenport, cradling it on her lap. "And good riddance," she laughed lightly.

"As I was saying," Jordan began again, "I've

had a change in plans. I've got to cancel tomorrow, but I should be in Frisco in about two weeks. How about dinner then?"

"Fine," Skye said shamelessly. She didn't even bother to look at her calendar; if other plans had been made, she'd cancel them. Being with Jordan was worth more than anything she could have scheduled.

"Oh, and while I'm thinking about it, give me the full name of that singer from the hospital again. I'd like to have Dan Murphy contact her. From the little I heard, the girl's got talent, exceptional talent."

"Dan Murphy?"

"He's the fellow who owns the radio station that employs yours truly."

"Oh." Skye had backed herself into a corner, forced to tell another white lie. "I told you her name is Jane, but honestly, Jordan, I don't think she's interested."

"You sound jealous." It was an accusation that rankled.

"That's ridiculous," she denied vehemently. "It's just that I find it disconcerting to have you phone me to ask about another woman."

They spoke for only a few minutes longer, the conversation suddenly stilted and unnatural. Skye replaced the receiver with a heavy heart. Her father had told her several years ago that *a liar is a fool who buries himself with deceit.* And here she was digging her own grave. Skye had always thought of herself as an honest person, yet somehow she had fallen into the habit of telling white lies. Had she been living a lie for so long that it had become second nature for her to utter half-truths indiscriminately? She had lied to herself and lied to God for eight years. Darn you, Jordan Kiley, she thought, for what you're doing to me, and bless you too, for forcing me into the light.

Skye didn't hear from Jordan the remainder of the week. She'd scheduled several projects for herself, including painting the kitchen and some spring cleaning, so her days were full and busy. Nonetheless, she couldn't help feeling disappointed that Jordan hadn't called. It had become of primary importance that she talk to him and explain her deception. She hadn't meant to lie, it had begun as a joke but had soon ballooned into a full-scale untruth.

Monday morning the children were happy and excited to be back in school. Skye had always loved children and was normally very patient, but by early afternoon she found herself snapping and fidgeting.

"How many times have I told you not to run in the classroom, David? How many?" she lashed out at the youngster from her desk.

Five-year-old David stared at her, his lower lip

quivering. "I'm sorry, Miss Garvin, I won't run again."

Yelling was no way to deal effectively with children, and Skye immediately felt guilty. "I'm sorry too, David, I shouldn't have shouted."

What had gotten into her to behave this way with the children? The answer was obvious. Misleading Jordan was weighing heavily on her mind, and she desperately needed to clear things between them.

Tuesday night, after fulfilling her volunteer duties, Skye remained later than usual waiting for Sally. A melody had been running through her mind most of the day, so while Sally finished up a few odds and ends Skye sat at the piano in the reception room. Slowly her fingers moved over the keys, transcribing the melody into notes. The pencil held in place by her mouth was jerked to and from its location countless times as she scratched the notes and marked new ones on the music sheet. Finally satisfied, she set the pencil down, ready to play the piece through.

The familiar sound of Sally's footsteps echoed from the back of the room.

"Listen to this," Skye commanded without turning, not wishing to break her concentration. Her fingers played the first chords of the intro-duction, filling the silent room with vibrating sound. The song had a natural rhythm and Skye stopped only once to change a single note. The music was bright and breezy, as her songs often were, with the kind of melodies that make people want to sing along and tap their feet. As the final notes faded, Skye smiled in satisfaction. A sense of accomplishment came over her. It was a good beginning, and the words were beginning to form in her mind.

"Sounds good, doesn't it?" she asked Sally, turning toward her friend.

But it wasn't Sally who stood behind her. "Jordan," she whispered in disbelief.

"Hello, *Jane,*" he said sarcastically. His mouth twisted into a hard, cruel line.

"Jordan, please . . ." Skye began, but stopped abruptly at the contempt she saw in his eyes.

"You lied." His voice grated. "After all your pretty, pompous talk, you lied." With that, he stalked from the room.

Chapter Six

"All right, kid, tell Aunt Sally all about it." It had only taken her perceptive friend three days to notice something was wrong.

"Tell you what?" Skye sipped lackadaisically on her herbal tea, feigning confusion.

"What's wrong, and don't try and tell me something isn't. I can tell just by looking at you that you're upset."

Skye laughed lightly. "Do I look any different?"

Sally studied her, shrewdly. "Yes, as a matter of fact, you do."

Crossing her eyes, Skye stuck out her tongue and laughed, but her laugh held little genuine amusement. "I'm exactly the same person I was the other day."

"No, you're not," Sally disputed soberly. "That sparkle is gone from your eyes. No . . . not sparkle, the expectation is missing. Did you and this John have a spat?"

Skye lowered her head, her hair falling forward to frame her oval face. "Sally, I'm not dating and never plan to date John Dirkson. He *is* my neighbor, but I misled you by insinuating there was something more between us. I . . . I also misled Jordan Kiley—but not about John—and when he discovered my game, well

. . . no one likes to be the butt of a joke."

Sally paused, waiting for Skye to elaborate, but when an explanation didn't follow, she probed. "Can't you make it right?"

Miserably Skye shook her head. There was no way of contacting him, and even if there were, Skye had decided not to. God had sent him into her life for a purpose, and that had been accomplished. But she would always be grateful to Jordan for removing the blinders that had hidden the truth.

"Hey," Sally interrupted her thoughts. "Didn't you tell me you were going out to dinner with Jordan Kiley next Friday night?"

"That's been canceled." At least Skye felt sure it must be. If by chance Jordan did happen to show, she wouldn't be home. It was Janey's birthday, and she was having dinner with her family.

"That's too bad, Skye, but I think meeting Jordan has done you a world of good."

Her lips trembled slightly as she attempted a smile. "I think you're right." Unexpectedly tears sprang to the surface and spilled down her cheek. Skye quickly wiped the moisture from her face before Sally noticed.

"With Jordan out of the picture maybe I could interest you in a blind date?"

How typical of the matchmaking Sally. Skye couldn't help but smile. "All right, you're on."

The contented grin of a Cheshire cat couldn't

have shown more satisfaction. "Steve King is a perfect match for you," Sally elaborated. "He's an accountant at Andy's firm; I know you're going to like him."

Skye had heard these identical words at least twenty times. But an accountant? She somehow pictured a tiny, bespectacled man with a fastidious nature. Biting her lip, she glanced at Sally hesitatingly.

"You're not backing out already, are you?"

"No," Skye said, "I was just wondering if it'd be too forward to ask him to help me balance my checkbook on our first date."

They both looked at one another and burst into giggles.

Skye was in much better spirits Thursday evening and played and sang for the children with a free-flowing happiness. Finishing, she turned to smile at her audience, but the smile froze on her face. Standing in the back of the room was Jordan. Had it only been nine days since she'd last seen him? It seemed a lifetime.

His steel gray eyes met the startled roundness of hers, pinning her. Sally glanced from one to the other and with a quiet efficiency moved the children and their families from the room.

Jordan waited until the room was nearly empty before advancing toward her. The wild hammering of her heart rushed a fresh supply of blood to her already flushed face. Her fingers remained poised over the piano keys and were trembling so badly she folded them awkwardly in her lap.

"Is it Jane or Skye?" he asked, devoid of emotion.

"Skye," she said in a breathy whisper. Nervously she moistened her lips. "Jordan, may I apologize? It was a stupid, childish prank, I . . ." She ran a shaky hand over her forehead, not sure if she should continue.

"Forget it," he said gruffly. "Is there somewhere we could go for coffee?"

Skye glanced pointedly at her watch, but if he'd asked her the time she couldn't have told him. "It's getting late. I think I should be heading home."

"Is the cafeteria open?"

"Yes, but . . ." she hesitated. If she was honest with herself, she'd admit she wanted to talk to him and clear away their misunderstanding.

His hand cupped her elbow possessively while she led the way to the elevator. The cafeteria was deserted, the kitchen area closed. Coffee and a few remaining desserts were sold on the honor system; a bowl sat atop the counter to collect the change. Jordan paid for the coffee while she carried their cups to a nearby table.

"Have you ever thought of becoming a professional singer?"

His question was so unexpected, she widened her eyes and wondered at his game. "No. I've never given the matter much thought."

"You're very gifted. You realize that, don't you?" The compliment was issued almost as a challenge.

Confusion invaded the blue depths of her eyes. This conversation was totally unexpected. Skye had hoped they could discuss their misunderstanding, not her singing ability.

"I'm not *that* talented," she insisted, and averted her face. His look was cold and hard, and she felt as if she barely knew him.

"I want to tape some of your music. I have a friend who owns a recording studio, and I'd like to have him listen to you." He watched her with amused contempt, as if anticipating a wild burst of enthusiasm at the generosity of his offer.

She gave him none. "I'm not interested. I'm honored that you think so highly of my talent, but no thanks."

His gaze narrowed in disbelief. "Don't lightly toss away this opportunity, Skye." His gaze seemed to question the rationale of her reasoning.

She sighed, releasing a jagged breath. How could she explain herself? Singing for the children was a joy, even an occasional solo with the church choir was a pleasurable challenge. But to make singing her life's work was out of the question. It didn't even tempt her.

She was given a respite by several nurses who entered the room. Their gaze rushed over her without notice and focused with interest upon

Jordan. She couldn't blame them; even with his broken arm, he managed to suggest a latent animal grace, his appeal totally masculine.

Jordan didn't even notice the interest he was generating, instead he continued to study Skye thoughtfully.

"Are you sure you've given this proper consideration?"

Nodding decisively, Skye said, "Quite sure."

Still he studied her, his bemusement keen.

Skye shifted uncomfortably. What a strange conversation this was. Glancing at her watch, she noted the time and quickly swallowed her coffee. "I must go," she said sadly. She had hoped to make things right between them, but it was clear Jordan wasn't interested.

His outstretched hand stopped her as she began to rise. The flint gray of his eyes pinned her to the seat. "I want you to give serious thought to my suggestion. It wouldn't hurt anything to make up a couple of tapes. You have the talent to make it, but the choice is yours."

Without so much as a second thought she shook her head. "I'm not going to change my mind. I never will." She stood then, and deposited her Styrofoam cup in the garbage on her way out the door.

The sad puppy cried pitifully when Skye replaced the barrier confining him to the kitchen. He had been frolicking between her feet and chewing on the bright, fuzzy slippers she wore. Large chocolate pools of misery watched as she petted him and whispered soothingly.

She would have to hurry and change clothes or she would be late for Janey's birthday dinner. But every time she left sight of the pup, he would yelp and howl. Twice John Dirkson had been over to complain about the noise. Skye had difficulty keeping her temper the second time, but smiled sweetly and promised to do her best. Her relationship with John had been strained and she wasn't sorry to hear he was moving at the end of the month.

With the puppy moderately quiet, she chose her most becoming new dress. The musky rose color accentuated the light tones of her hair, while the soft gathers at the waist emphasized her willowy suppleness. She'd finished fastening the button-loop closure down the front and knotting the tie when the doorbell rang.

Could it be Jordan? This was the night they had set their dinner date, but he had been so forbidding and phlegmatic the day before. No, it wouldn't be him but perhaps someday God would send him back into her life and she could make her amends. She finished buckling the strap of her shoe and hobbled across her living room, one shoe on, one shoe off. It must be John to complain about the pup again.

It wasn't. "Jordan," she breathed, feeling stiff and nervous.

"Hello. May I come in?" he asked. His eyes widened in appreciation as he did an appraising sweep of her appearance.

Still suffering the effects of surprise, she stepped aside. "Of course; I'm sorry."

He moved past her into the living room, his eyes warm and amused as he watched her.

"I didn't think you were coming," she began unevenly.

"Did I say I wasn't?" His eyes left hers momentarily and fell upon the puppy confined in her kitchen. "Your burglar alarm system?" he joked casually. "I see. Once warned, you attack the intruder, using your shoe as a weapon." A crooked smile turned up the edges of his mouth as he glanced at the high heel sandal in her hand.

"Of course not." Her step faltered slightly as she slipped the shoe on as gracefully as possible.

"Aren't you forgetting something?"

"What?"

"Your money? I'd hate to see you leave home without it."

"Why are you here?" she asked him breathlessly, confused.

"I thought we had a date."

"I . . . I didn't think you meant to keep it." Skye knew she wouldn't be able to maintain this pretense of self-possession much longer.

"You've made other arrangements." It was a statement full of contempt.

It would be easy to lie again, let him assume another half-truth. He would go then, and she knew with an unexplainable certainty that she wouldn't see him again.

"It's my niece's birthday. I was going to have dinner with my family. Janey's nine today."

"Ahh . . . Jane, that's where you got the name."

"My given name is Jane too." She sat directly opposite him, pausing to buckle her shoe while gathering the courage to explain her lies. "Jordan, I don't remember how the whole thing started, letting you believe the singer was someone else. I've felt terrible all week."

"Let's forget it," he said tightly.

"I don't want to forget it, and I doubt that I'll be able to until I explain myself. I didn't mean to mislead you. I'm not even sure why I did. Maybe it was because I didn't want to talk about myself that first night. Or perhaps I wanted you to like me for myself, not for any talent I may possess. Can you understand that?"

His probing eyes swept over her. "Yes, I can."

"I don't want you to accept my apology. I want you to forgive me. There's a difference. I need your forgiveness, Jordan."

He stood and came to her side. Gently he brought her upright, easing her against his body.

117

Kissing her hair, his hand gently stroked her arm. "I forgive you," he whispered huskily.

Skye's arms slid effortlessly around him, her mouth turning instinctively toward his. As his lips fit over hers a searing contentment stole over her. It felt so right to be in his arms. He shuddered against her, and Skye nestled her head upon his broad shoulder.

"Have dinner with me?" he mumbled into her hair.

"I want to," she admitted huskily, "but I can't. My family is waiting for me."

Raising her face, he kissed her again with an infinite tenderness, arching her toward him.

"You could come with me," she whispered. "Brad and Peggy won't mind." Her lovely mouth curved into an appealing smile. "Besides, I'm going to need help with the pup."

Jordan chuckled softly. "Scheming woman, aren't you?"

Her car had no sooner pulled up alongside the curb when Janey came rushing from the house and down the front steps. The screen door slammed behind her only to be opened again a few seconds later.

"It's about time you got here," Brad scolded affectionately, and then noticed Jordan, who came around the other side of the car. "So this is the reason you're late," he teased her in a brotherly manner.

"Don't embarrass me," she joked, but her eyes were serious.

"Would I do a thing like that?" he asked laughingly.

The two men shook hands after an informal introduction and walked toward the house talking companionably. Skye and Peggy rescued the pup from the back seat of her car while Janey squealed with delight over her birthday gift.

While the men sat in the living room talking, Skye helped Peggy finish the salad and add an extra place at the table.

"I hope you don't mind my bringing Jordan unexpectedly," Skye said as she glanced into the living room and saw how well Jordan got along with her brother.

Peggy's smile was full of warmth. "Of course not," she denied instantly. "I was dying to meet him anyway."

"Is Jordan your boyfriend, Aunt Skye?" Janey quizzed as she lopped a fingerful of frosting from the cake.

"Hey, you!" Peggy cried. "Keep your greedy finger off the cake."

"Is he?" She repeated her question.

Skye wasn't sure how to answer. A contentment flowed through her and unconsciously she found herself studying Jordan from the kitchen. Lean and powerful, he sat with his long legs stretched before him exuding an aura of strength.

"Auntie Skye?" Janey grabbed Skye's hand as if to pull her attention back to herself.

"I'm sorry, Cupcake." Skye broke her concentration. "Yes, I guess you could say he's my boyfriend." But she didn't want her niece to pursue the subject further. "How do you like the puppy?"

"He's wonderful. . . . I think I'll name him Samson. What do you think?"

"It's a great idea," Skye said, hugging her.

The meal was an enjoyable sharing time. Everyone participated in the laughter and teasing.

"I'm stuffed." Brad leaned back in his chair and patted his stomach.

"You better have room for dessert," Janey warned, not wanting to delay opening her gifts.

"I think I've managed to save a little room for cake. How about you, Jordan?"

"I've always got room for birthday cake." He purposely winked at Janey, who dissolved into delighted giggles.

Skye rose after Peggy, conscious of Jordan's warm gaze following her. "I'll help Peggy with the cake," she said as if needing an excuse to leave.

They returned a few minutes later carrying in the cake with nine lighted candles and singing the traditional birthday song.

"Make your wish, Princess," Brad prompted.

Janey closed her eyes tightly, then announced excitedly, "I wished for a baby brother."

Standing behind his wife, Brad laughed. "I don't

know." His arms slid contentedly around Peggy's still flat stomach. "I wouldn't object to another girl. It's not many men who can claim to live in a harem of beautiful women." Playfully he nuzzled Peggy's neck, making growling noises.

The gifts were opened, including the necklace Skye had bought with Jordan the first night they'd gone to dinner. Janey also got a new game and a pair of pajamas.

The adults moved into the living room, and when Skye brought Jordan his coffee, his arm circled her waist, bringing her down to sit on the arm of his chair. His grip held her there, his eyes smiling into hers.

"Where's Brad?" she asked, returning his warm gaze with one of her own.

"He's gone to phone for a taxi. My flight is leaving soon."

Skye's heart floundered at his casual announcement. "Already?" she asked hesitantly, and swallowed convulsively at the knot forming in her throat. She wanted to look away, afraid he would read her disappointment, but his gaze held hers.

"Come to the airport with me?" he asked.

"Okay," she returned lightly, although her smile wavered dangerously. "I . . . I can drive us."

"I'd rather take the taxi." Jordan's arm tightened around her waist.

A short time later the cab was there and waiting. They said their good-byes on the porch. Jordan and Brad grasped hands with the familiarity of good friends.

Skye hugged both Peggy and Janey. "I hope you had a very special birthday, Cupcake."

"Oh, Auntie Skye, I really did," Janey assured her. "And I like Jordan a lot."

"I'd be more than willing to drive you to the airport," Brad offered, but the look he exchanged with Jordan showed he understood his wish to be alone with Skye.

Within a few minutes they were on their way. Brad, Peggy and Janey stood on the porch waving; Skye focused her attention on the fading figures as long as possible.

Jordan was strangely quiet, as if there were something on his mind. Skye more than carried the conversation, babbling inanities that were totally irrelevant to anything.

The reality of his leaving hit forcefully when they approached the airport. Skye could no longer deny the tears burning for release. This was stupid, why was she crying? A lone tear forced itself free and rolled down her cheek. Fiercely she brushed it away before Jordan could notice.

The walk down the concourse seemed like twenty miles; Skye chatted continuously.

Stopping her abruptly, Jordan gently touched her wet cheek. "Why are you crying?" he asked with tender concern.

"I am?" she questioned. "Oh, I always cry when

I'm happy." She'd promised God and herself she'd never lie again, but her resolve crumbled under the first attack of pride. "I've never been so happy," she said in a kind of desperation. "Peggy's pregnant, Janey's birthday . . . and look at you, Mr. Grinch, your arm is healing and . . ." A bubble of laughter quickly became a sob.

The concourse and airline gate was crowded with people waiting to board the plane. Jordan maneuvered Skye to a far corner offering them as much privacy as possible.

"I've listened to your Pollyanna chatter all the way here. Now, I'll ask you again—why are you crying?" His hand gripped her arm painfully, the line of his jaw tight and controlled.

Everything suddenly went very still; the wall he backed her against felt hard and unyielding. Skye held her breath, concentrating on the top of his shoe. She didn't know what had gotten into her. She was normally a very composed woman.

"Skye," he groaned impatiently, and his finger lifted her chin to read her watery blue eyes. "Please tell me why you're crying," his low voice coaxed as he gathered her into his arms. Her softness molded against him, welcoming the comfort of his embrace. His hand rubbed her back in a soothing, circular motion.

Held protectively, Skye accepted the solid strength and buried her face in his shirt, allowing the tears to flow.

"I'm sorry," she attempted in apology. "I'm being ridiculous." She could feel the gentle pressure of his lips kiss her hair.

"No, you're not," his own voice sounded strained and faintly raw.

"Oh, Jordan, I don't honestly know why I'm crying. I can't believe how stupid I'm being."

An announcement came from the loudspeaker, and Jordan stiffened, mumbling a curse. "That's my flight," he said impatiently. But he didn't relax the taut grip of his arm shaping her against him. When he did lift his head, an expanding frown darkened his expression.

Skye stared back wordlessly, but when she tried to pull away he caught her shoulder, fixing his gaze upon hers. With a fierce kind of gentleness, he cupped her face, his mouth seeking hers.

When the amplified voice was repeated, he slowly released her, his hand caressing the softness of her face.

"I've got to go." The emotion in his voice was so ragged it startled Skye.

A frail smile formed. "I know." Using the back of her hand, she wiped the remaining tears aside. She studied him, putting to memory every detail of his rugged face.

"I didn't mean to blubber all over your shirt." She wiped his chest, as if to erase the wet stains her tears had made.

His eyes regarded her with a languorous

warmth. Glancing over his shoulder, he noted there were only a few people left in line boarding the plane.

"There are things I want to tell you," he admitted with forced patience. "And now all I can think about is how long it's going to be before I can kiss you again, or run my fingers through your hair." Quickly he checked the progress of the receding line and jerked his attention back to her. "If I fly back next weekend, will you be here?"

"Yes." Her voice sounded choked and small. Then, gaining verbal strength, she repeated, "Yes, of course I'll be here."

They began to ease their way toward the jetway. Everyone had now boarded and only the steward remained.

"I have to go," Jordan said, gazing deep into her eyes.

"I know." Fresh tears misted over her eyes, and her mouth trembled in an effort to smile.

"I'll phone you," he promised, backing away from her.

"Okay, good-bye, Jordan. God go with you," she finally managed to say, her voice a tortured whisper. She watched him disappear into the long jetway that ushered him inside the plane.

She remained for a long time looking onto the brightly lit runway several minutes after his plane had made its ascension into the night.

Lost in a whirlwind of reflection, Skye reached

the parking garage before realizing she hadn't brought her car with her. Releasing a long, irritated breath, she made her way outside the terminal hoping to flag down a cab. She was no sooner outside when one of the drivers who was leaning against the side of the building straightened and came forward.

"Here you are, miss." He smiled wide in greeting.

It was the driver who had brought them from Brad's. "You waited for me?" she asked incredulously.

"Yes, ma'am," he assured her. "Your man wanted to be absolutely certain you were taken home safely." His crooked grin and beaming eyes revealed he had been well paid for his services.

The driver let her out in front of Brad's and waited until her car had started and she was on her way before leaving. Skye knew Brad and Peggy had probably waited up for her, but she didn't feel like facing them tonight. She had too many feelings to deal with. What had caused her to act as she had? She couldn't remember doing anything so stupid in her life. Anyone would have thought he was going off to war instead of returning home. It was amazing he was interested in her at all. She had bungled this relationship from the beginning. She had teased him, promised and misled him, lied to him, ranted and raved at him and now acted like a complete idiot.

She sat on her bed reading from her Bible, sorting through her feelings and discussing this relationship in prayer when the phone rang.

Jordan. It had to be him; no one else would phone this late.

"Hello." She didn't attempt to disguise the eagerness in her voice.

"You're home!" came the obvious observation. "Where have you been all night? I've tried phoning several times."

"Hello, Sally," she tried to hide her disappointment, but the unnatural dip in her voice revealed her letdown. "I was at my niece's birthday dinner." She didn't add that Jordan had gone with her.

"I should have remembered that," Sally chastised herself. "Were you expecting a call from someone else? You sound disappointed."

"No, not really," Skye said. "What's up?" Sally wouldn't phone unless it was something important, not this late at any rate.

"I've got some marvelous news. I knew you'd want to know right away. You don't mind my calling this late, do you?"

Leave it to Sally to keep her dangling with anticipation. "You know I don't. Now, what's so all-fired important?"

"Dr. Warren was in this afternoon and he feels Billy has a slim chance of walking again."

"What? Are you kidding?" Skye gasped in disbelief. It wasn't a serious question. Sally wouldn't jest about Billy's future. The question was a natural outpouring of her own incredulity.

"A colleague of Dr. Warren's from back East—I think his name is Snell—has been doing some experimental surgery in cases like Billy's," she continued, listing the specific areas of the spine now operable under the new technique, but the technical terms flew over Skye's head.

"Yes . . . yes, but what does all this mumbo jumbo mean?" Skye interrupted.

Sally laughed. "I was getting to that. What all this boils down to is the fact that there's a possibility this new technique will work in Billy's case. Dr. Snell is flying here for some medical conference, and he's agreed to examine Billy and determine the feasibility of success. If—and it's a big if—Billy's found to be a low-risk candidate, he'll undergo the surgery."

"Oh, Sally, I've prayed for something like this."

"You're not crying, are you?" Sally accused, her own elated voice wobbling with suppressed tears.

"No, silly, these aren't tears, this is liquid joy."

Chapter Seven

Monday and Tuesday passed in a dull shade of expectancy. Even though her days and nights were full, Skye found several things she wanted to share with Jordan. Little things. She'd finally broken a seven-minute mile, a goal she'd set for herself a year before. And of course she wanted to tell him about Billy. And there was one thing he must know that was sure to displease him.

Wednesday afternoon Skye unlocked her apartment door, slipped off her shoes and entered her bedroom to change clothes, a pattern so set it was almost like instinct. She turned on her radio, a sound to fill the silence. Funny, she'd never thought of music like that before. Music had been her panacea, filling the void in her life, offering challenge and purpose. Suddenly it had become a sound to fill the silence.

Later she lay with her head resting against the back of the davenport. Had she fallen in love with Jordan? Was all this longing for the sound of his voice and the coming weekend *love?* She cupped her tea mug with her long, slender fingers and sipped it absently. Her feelings for Glen had been so different from this. With Glen she'd felt cherished and protected. But Jordan drew from her something totally different. Something almost indefinable; a strong, fierce emotion. She shook her head to dispel her thoughts, unwilling to continue in this senseless vein.

Intent on reading her book, she tucked her bare feet beneath her and placed her mug down just as the phone rang.

"Hello," she said cheerfully.

"Hello, Skye."

"Jordan," she breathed his name, and her heart skipped a beat. "I'm so glad you called. I was beginning to think my watery charades had convinced you I was a candidate for the looney bin."

His laughter was full and rich. "The thought crossed my mind the first time you took off your shoe."

Skye tightened her grip on the receiver, as if it would make what she had to say easier. "I have some bad news and some good news; which do you want first?"

He didn't even pause. "I learned a long time ago to deal with any unpleasantness first."

"When I got home last week," she began hesitantly, "I looked on my calendar and I noticed that . . . that I've already got a date for this Saturday night. I . . . promised Sally I'd meet a friend of her husband's."

Jordan was silent for so long, Skye wondered if he was still on the line. "Jordan?" her voice wobbled.

"Break it," he demanded harshly.

"I can't. I want to, but Sally has gone to a lot of trouble, and I did promise . . ." she finished lamely.

Jordan's voice was sharp with anger. "I really don't care about hurting your friend's feelings."

"Please try and understand," she pleaded, her voice hoarse with the effort. "It's not like a real date. I haven't even met this guy. Sally's been trying to fix this up for weeks. I can't let her down now."

The quiet was tense and oppressive.

"Just what do you expect me to do? Jump for joy?"

"No." The word came out squeaky and high-pitched. "I . . . I was hoping we could spend Saturday together, and as much of Sunday as your schedule will allow."

"You can't honestly expect me to come?" he asked forcefully.

"If you don't, I think I'll go crazy." She hadn't meant to reveal so much of her feelings, to admit quite that much.

He sighed heavily, and when he spoke, the grim anger had left. "I think I would too," he admitted huskily.

The tight constriction left her throat. "We'll have a wonderful day," she breathed softly.

"Unfortunately it was the night I was looking forward to."

"Then I'll have to thank my guardian angel for looking after me," she said light-heartedly.

She could hear pages being flipped, as if he were consulting an appointment calendar. "What about Friday night?"

Skye had already made plans with the church youth group. "I . . . I kind of have something going that night," she said, more than a little apprehensive. "What time could you be here?"

"Around seven."

She sighed softly. "Praise God, that'll work out great. Eat a light dinner, because we're having hot fudge sundaes afterward."

"After what?"

"You'll see," she laughed lightly. "It'll be fun, I promise."

A male voice interrupted from the background. It sounded vaguely like Bill Malloy, the man Skye had met the day her car broke down.

"I've got to go," he groaned impatiently.

"Jordan, I have some wonderful news about Billy. I'll tell you Friday. Good-bye. God go with you."

"Friday at seven," he said in a husky voice that sounded very much like a promise.

Skye had no sooner hung up the phone when it rang again. It was Janey. "Auntie Skye," she burst out excitedly. "Can you come over right away? I've got something to show you."

Skye glanced quickly at her watch; there was

plenty of time before church. "All right, Cupcake."

Brad and Peggy were doing yard work when she drove up. Janey saw her from down the street and came racing up the sidewalk.

"Come see," she yelled, running with all her strength.

Brad rose from the flower bed he was weeding to meet her. "Yes, come see," he encouraged with sparkling eyes.

Janey grabbed her hand, breathless from the run. "It arrived this morning. I was so surprised."

"Hey, you guys," Skye laughed, her brow furrowed. "What gives?"

Tugging fiercely at Skye's hand, Janey led the way around the back of the house. When Brad and Peggy followed, Skye glanced skeptically over her shoulder, thoroughly confused.

Once they rounded the corner, her gaze caught a large brown doghouse. Built to resemble a miniature home, it contained white shutters beside two windows. SAMSON was painted in bookhand above the door. Squatting down, Skye could see that plush carpeting covered the floor except for a small space of linoleum in the kitchen area that was used for the dog's water and food dishes.

Samson slumbered peacefully inside his new quarters and Skye petted the puppy with long, flowing strokes.

"Brad, it's a darling house. Where did you ever find it?" she asked over her shoulder.

"I didn't!"

Her eyes widened and swept his controlled expression, but Brad only smiled back. Janey was no help either. Obviously primed for silence, she pinched her lips closed with her fingers.

"Peggy?" Skye turned her questioning eyes to her sister-in-law.

"Jordan had it delivered this morning," Peggy said at last, recognizing Skye's frustration.

"Jordan did?" A warm bubble of happiness surfaced.

"Take some friendly advice," Brad said pensively. "Hold on to Jordan Kiley. He's a rare man."

Her smile was tremulous, but her eyes sparkled with a light of contentment and promise. "I think I will," she said.

"Aren't you going to tell Aunt Skye the best news of all?" Janey demanded from inside the doghouse. Samson was cradled on her lap and looking disgruntled because his nap and his home had been invaded.

"What news?" Skye's attention swiveled back to her brother. "You got a job!" She really didn't need to guess further, nothing else could have removed the lines of doubt and worry that had furrowed his expression for weeks. He even seemed to stand taller, as if some heavy load had been lifted from him.

"I start Monday morning." A grin lit up his boyish face.

"And more money than we dared dream," Peggy interjected enthusiastically.

"The Lord works in mysterious ways. Funny, I never expected to get that job." Brad opened the back door leading to the kitchen. "Come inside and I'll tell you all about it."

The three adults entered the house, leaving Janey contentedly behind, sitting in the doghouse.

The bus was loaded with thirty-five laughing, teasing junior high students. The festive mood intensified as Skye and Jordan climbed aboard with the bus driver.

"All right, kids." Skye stood in the front of the bus, calling them to attention. "Hold it down a minute while I go over the rules and introduce you to my friend. This is Mr. Kiley, and he'll be accompanying us tonight."

A chorus of hoots and welcomes came from the lively group.

Jordan acknowledged their acceptance with a casual wave of his hand.

"I see you had to twist his arm to come," one of the boys from the back of the bus shouted, referring to his broken arm.

Other jeers followed laughter. "Robert, be careful, I may have to twist your mouth," Skye said, returning the banter easily.

After reviewing the rules Skye sat beside Jordan in one of the front seats of the bus. The driver started the vehicle and pulled out of the parking lot, while the eager bunch sang songs accompanied by Skye on the guitar. What they lacked in talent was more than compensated for in volume.

The theater parking lot was packed with cars and several other church buses. Some discussion followed on how to locate their bus after the movie.

"Just remember ours is the yellow one," Jordan offered.

"Cute, fellow."

"Funny."

"Who is this guy, Don Rickles?" came a sprinkling of wisecracks.

Although the Christian film's message was geared toward their charges, Skye prayed fervently that Jordan would respond to the invitation to accept Christ as his personal Savior. At the end of the film the invocation was repeated by counselors at the front of the theater. Several boys and girls went forward.

Skye tipped her head back to watch Jordan, but his expression was closed and unreadable. Sighing inwardly, she realized that for Jordan, placing his trust in Christ would not come easily. Independence and self-reliance were so much a part of his personality, Skye wondered how long it would take him to recognize his need. From what she knew of him, Jordan would investigate Christianity thoroughly before making a commitment. Skye desperately wanted him to know and love Christ as she did. There was no denying the growing attraction she felt for Jordan, and it was of primary importance that he share her deep faith.

Feeling her gaze touch him, Jordan turned, his eyes regarding her seriously. They narrowed suddenly, as if reading the question in her eyes. His mouth thinned, and she knew she had displeased him.

I must be patient, she told herself. I must learn to let the Holy Spirit do the calling.

Hot fudge sundaes waited for them back at the church. No one needed encouragement to dig in. Jordan and Skye sat opposite one another at the long tables. Although they sat among several teens, the numbers didn't lessen the sense of intimacy between them. Several times she found Jordan watching her curiously, but she avoided his gaze, joking with the kids around her instead.

Jordan finished his ice cream and pushed the bowl aside.

"You're not done, are you?" Skye asked incredulously. Jordan had eaten the vanilla ice cream but had left the chocolate syrup. Not waiting for his answer, she took his bowl and poured the chocolate over her ice cream. "I know, I know," she joked, "once on the lips, forever on the hips. But I'm going to splurge. I have a weakness for chocolate."

Jordan's smile seemed to reach out and touch

her. "I have a weakness too," he admitted, his eyes focused on her full mouth. "But my weakness lies in the area of blue-eyed blondes who sing like angels and hide cash from muggers in their shoes."

Thick lashes quickly veiled her reaction, but his words brought a curious sensation to her heart.

Before she could find a witty comment to trade with him, the tables and chairs began to vibrate. Bowls of ice cream shimmied across the tabletop.

Someone yelled, "Earthquake." But no one moved, each paralyzed, their eyes filled with panic.

Skye had experienced several minor earthquakes in her lifetime, but nothing that seemed to be this strong. The crucifix suspended from the ceiling by two wires swayed as the room rocked. Several bowls had reached the end of the table and were ready to crash to the floor. Skye jerked herself upright to catch them, but in the rush lost her footing. She felt herself fall, the floor rushing up to meet her. Everything went black, although she was conscious.

Then it was over, everything was still. She remained frozen until she was roughly jerked into Jordan's arms.

"Dear God," he moaned into her hair, "are you all right?" Skye didn't care that his cast was biting unmercifully into her ribs. She clung to him as the only solid thing in a reeling world.

People began to move around; some of the girls were crying, still caught in the terror.

"I'm okay." Her first breaths came in gasps. "I must have hit my head. Everything went black for a couple of seconds, but I'm okay now."

Jordan's look burned her, his eyes a brilliant shade of silver. Urgently his hand pushed the hair away from her face, as if needing some reassurance she wasn't injured.

Besides the fright, no one had been hurt, and what had seemed an eternity wasn't any more than five seconds.

In the aftermath everyone started to speak at once. Someone started singing a chorus of praise and thanksgiving, others joined and soon the whole group was lifting their voices in gratitude to a merciful God. Everyone except Jordan, who remained detached and cynical.

Silently they rode home in Jordan's rented car. He had hardly spoken since the quake. The radio was full of the news, stating that the quake's epicenter had originated miles away, as was often, fortunately, the case.

Sitting beside him, Skye could see that his mouth was tight; his hand clenched the steering wheel, rigid and white. He pulled up in front of her apartment building and turned off the engine.

"Are you sure you're all right?" he asked again gruffly. He didn't look at her; his profile, bathed in the moonlight, showed his jaw to be flexing.

"I'm fine," she insisted shakily.

Jordan expelled his breath forcefully. "Thank God."

"Yes, I do! Thank Him, that is." That Jordan should be so affected by what had happened brought an odd, breathless quality to her voice. She paused, unsure why she was asking him the question. "Would it have mattered to you if I'd been hurt?" Perhaps she needed assurance that this magnetic attraction was mutual.

His laugh was harsh and cold. "Yes, it matters."

A puzzled frown marred her expression. What was wrong? He had been acting strangely ever since the quake. "Jordan, why are you so angry?"

He was silent for so long, Skye wondered if he'd heard her. "Jordan?" she repeated.

When he did turn toward her, his eyes were as hard as forged iron. "Maybe I don't like the way I feel about you. Maybe I wished I could put you out of my mind and find someone who lived in the real world. You Christians, you think reading the Bible and mumbling a few prayers is going to solve everything."

His attack was so unexpected, Skye drew her breath in sharply.

"Well, I think it's time you woke up, Pollyanna. You could have been killed tonight."

"So what!" she spat angrily. "That isn't the worst thing that could happen to me. I might have blocked Christ out of my life, I might never have known God's love." *Or yours,* she added silently. "But . . . but, you're right about one thing, Jordan Kiley," she said, her voice wobbling, "maybe it is time I woke up." Angrily she jerked open the car door.

"Skye," the grim authority in his voice stopped her. "I wouldn't, if I were you."

"May I remind you this is the real world. I'll do darn well as I please." With a quickness born of hurt and resentment, she jerked herself upright, ready to slam the car door.

"Skye, please." His voice was an odd mixture of fury and pleading.

Unsure, she paused, taking several breaths to release the tension.

Both were silent for several minutes.

Finally Jordan opened his car door and stood. "Invite me in for coffee."

Numbly she nodded.

Neither of them was interested in coffee, although Skye made the pretense of putting water on to boil. "All I have is instant."

"Fine," he muttered.

She stood with her back to him in the kitchen waiting for the kettle to whistle before pouring their coffee. She didn't want to face Jordan, not yet.

Suddenly he was there, behind her. Skye could feel his breath stirring her hair; then his hand cupped her shoulder, pulling her against him.

Weakly Skye submitted to the potency of his unspoken command. Without self-directing thought she turned, her arms sliding around him, his chest a cushion where she could hear the ragged pounding of his heart. His fingers tunneled through her hair, molding her head against him.

"Forgive me," he spoke at last, his voice raspy.

Skye smiled secretly to herself. Jordan had asked her forgiveness, instead of saying he was sorry. She lifted her face, her eyes meeting his. She understood his message.

His finger lightly touched her lips before lifting her chin to meet his descending mouth. The kiss began gently and fleetingly but deepened until Jordan shuddered and firmly closed his mouth over hers. When his tongue outlined her lips, Skye groaned and moved away slightly. They were tampering with temptations beyond their strength.

"Skye," he groaned into her hair. "I think you better pour us that coffee."

Still dazed, she blinked her round eyes.

"Would you like me to do it?" He brought down two mugs from the cupboard, more in command of his senses than she.

"I'll . . . I'll pour, thanks." She was composed by the time she brought their coffee into the living room. "Before I forget, Janey needs your address. She wants to write you a thank-you note. It was thoughtful of you to buy her such a nice gift."

"My pleasure." He took the pen and pad from the coffee table and scribbled a few lines in bold, even strokes.

"How much time do we have tomorrow before your date?" Jordan demanded, and frowned.

"All day, really." She wasn't looking forward to this blind date. "Sally said I should be ready around seven thirty."

He nodded, his brows knitting together in an expression of disapproval.

"Can we go sailing tomorrow?" She didn't want to end the evening with another argument and hoped to steer their conversation away from any unpleasantness. "Brad and I share ownership in a small twenty-one-foot sloop. I think you'll like it."

Jordan grinned and gave an approving nod. "As long as it's understood I'm the captain and you're the crew."

"Yes, sir," she saluted him enthusiastically.

"I'll tolerate no insubordination," he said crisply.

"None, sir."

A grin twitched at the corners of his mouth. "I could get to like this. All right, your first command is to walk me to the door and kiss me good night."

"Right away, sir." She did as he requested, and by the time Jordan left the only thing cool was their coffee.

• • •

"If I take the wings of the dawn. If I dwell in the remotest part of the sea, even there Thy hand will guide me and Thy right hand will take hold of me."

"What are you mumbling?" Jordan's words shot past her in the brisk wind.

"Nothing," she mumbled. Prying her hand loose from the mast, she gave him a tiny wave of reassurance, then grabbed hold again in a death grip.

Once the sails were up, the sailboat immediately keeled, and Skye fought the sensation she would fall overboard. "Dear Lord," she prayed, "just get me out of this *alive.*" Her mind whirled with the wind. All she needed to do now was tie off the sails in an eight-knot. But how does an eight-knot go? Every sailor's daughter knows how to tie something so simple. How could she have forgotten? Everything fell into place suddenly, and Skye sighed in relief.

She crawled on all fours back to Jordan in the cockpit, her heart in her throat.

He seemed to be finding her escapades very amusing, and there was no disguising the laughter in his eyes.

"We've got a good brisk wind," he said as she lowered herself to safety.

"A brisk wind?" she said incredulously. "I've seen hurricanes of less force."

"I thought you said you were an experienced sailor." His eyes were beaming with a wicked, teasing light.

"It was only a slight exaggeration," Skye said, defending herself. "I sailed with Brad and my father several times. I may even have managed to raise the sails once or twice, but never in winds like this."

Jordan laughed and motioned for her to join him. Skye went readily; fitting into his arms seemed to come naturally. Expertly Jordan maneuvered the helm through the open waters.

"What were you mumbling up there? You looked very intent."

Lifting a strand of wind-driven hair from her face, she laughed. "I was talking to God, reminding Him that He said His right hand would guide me. I felt I needed it up there."

Some of the amusement left his eyes. "Do you always talk to God?"

"Sure, that's what's known as prayer." She smiled absently, enjoying the sensation of slicing through the water. It freed her spirit and lifted her soul.

"You really believe in this Jesus stuff, don't you?" His expression was thoughtful as he met her gaze.

"With all my heart." Her look, more than her words, stated the depth of her faith. "Is it so difficult for you to believe Jesus is God's Son?"

Jordan was quiet, as if turning the question over in his mind. Skye could see he was uncomfortable. "From the evidence that exists, Christ lived on earth. Whether He was who He said He was is another matter."

"Not if you examine the facts." Skye didn't want to be pushy. She had learned long ago that Christ is a gentleman who didn't barge into someone's life. He came only when invited.

"I guess what I don't understand is that you all seem to think God is so good, but look at all the evil and bad things that happen."

"That is difficult, isn't it? I think one of the hardest things for me to accept as a Christian has been the belief that everything that happens to me is for my good."

Jordan gave a small unpleasant laugh. "Don't try and tell me that crippling Billy was doing the poor kid a favor."

"No, but you're missing an important point. God didn't cause Billy's accident. He did allow it to happen, but ultimately it will be for Billy's good. A Christian must see that in every situation."

"My God," he responded mockingly. "You really are a Pollyanna. Wasn't that her game? The glad game? Finding something good in every situation."

Averting her face, Skye could feel a lump forming in her throat. "I guess it does sound childish to you, Jordan, but I've put absolute trust in my God, and I must believe that whatever happens to me or those I love is for the best."

Jordan sighed, his look pensive. "Then I think we should agree to disagree."

A brooding unhappiness settled over Skye. How could their relationship continue if Jordan differed so strongly with her religious views? With an upward sweep of her lashes, Skye glanced at him. His dark gray eyes were masked and troubled. Skye yearned to reach out and touch him, to answer the doubts that plagued him. The need crescendoed until she thought she would weep with the agony of it. She wanted to trust God, longed for that intense faith that would raise her above her own doubts. Instead she sat beside him depressed and weary. Unexpectedly the sun broke through the heavy clouds, offering promise. Skye's spirits soared; she needed a promise, something to hold on to until Jordan recognized the truth. Smiling, Skye turned her face heavenward in silent communication. She was ready to trust.

"Hey, how about a sandwich?" she asked, feeling the need to lighten the mood. "I'm starved."

Jordan's gaze swept slowly over her face. "All right, how about a ham on rye with mustard, mayo and pickles?"

"Yes, sir," she responded with a twinkle in her eye. "One peanut butter and jelly coming up."

The sound of his amusement followed her as she went below.

The mood became more serious as their discussion continued on other subjects. Although their opinions varied, and they were just as prone to argue over something as agree, their differences were not so far removed. Except for one—Christ.

Jordan's knowledge of music surprised Skye, and she noted how he cleverly steered the conversation to her singing.

"You have a marvelous talent," he reminded her. "I'd like for you to reconsider my offer and let Dan Murphy listen to you."

Skye laughed and dismissed his offer with a shrug.

"You can be persistent, can't you? Singing for money would take all the fun out of it for me. Besides, I already am a professional."

His eyes widened curiously.

"Teacher," Skye added.

"Do you enjoy teaching that much?"

Dragging her fingertips along the surface of the water, Skye straightened. "There are days I wonder, but then I've always loved children, and teaching is what I do best."

"You actually enjoy children?" He made it sound like a character defect.

"I'm a teacher, I'd better," she told him adamantly. "I think the younger the better. It's difficult for me to watch Janey grow up. I see her developing into a young woman and it tears at my soul. I don't want her to become independent and self-reliant. In the beginning it was almost as if Janey were my own child. She's named after me, you know." Skye laughed at his expression. "Poor kid, getting stuck with an ordinary name like Jane."

His eyes held hers with mocking reproach. "There's nothing plain about you. But if you're so keen on children, why don't you have one?"

"I will, if I marry."

"In case you haven't heard, a girl doesn't need to be married to have a baby," he countered quickly, some of the teasing gone from his voice.

"This girl does."

"I see, it's like choking down your vegetables before being allowed to sample the delights of dessert."

Her eyes fell, avoiding his. "If that's the way you want to look at it. Do you find marriage so objectionable?"

His facial muscles softened, and the smile he gave her was warm and gentle. "No. As a matter of fact, I agree with you. I wanted to get married once, but the lady was more interested in a career than in a family—or in committing herself to one man, for that matter."

The woman had been mad, Skye decided, to reject Jordan's love. "Do you still love her?" Where the question came from, Skye didn't know; it just popped out. Just thinking Jordan loved another brought a sharp pain to her midsection.

"No. Whatever I felt for her died long ago."

Skye risked a glance at Jordan and relaxed.

"Do you still love him?" Jordan asked unexpectedly.

"Who?"

"The one you've been eating your heart over."

Confused and unsure of how to respond, Skye looked away. "Yes, I guess I do."

Jordan's eyes became grim and cold, and Skye realized she couldn't leave it there. "He was killed in a car accident eight years ago." Her voice was tight yet soft, indicating the emotion the simple words had cost her.

Jordan's expression softened, followed by surfacing compassion. "I'm sorry."

Her smile was weak. "So am I."

An hour later they docked the sloop at the marina.

"What about tomorrow?" Jordan questioned as they strolled toward her apartment.

"There's church in the morning," she announced casually. "I'm singing with the choir. Would you like to come?"

"Yes, I would," he stated softly.

His response surprised her in more ways than one. She'd expected him to complain because of their limited time together. "Praise God," she murmured silently, "He's working already."

Willingly Skye turned into Jordan's arms the minute her apartment door was closed.

"Take this with you tonight," he mumbled huskily. The hard possession of his mouth brought physical pain. Her tender lips felt bruised and swollen under the force of his kiss, but it didn't seem to matter. She understood his fierce hunger.

Chapter Eight

I enjoyed myself." Steve King stood in the hallway outside Skye's apartment. His gaze freely roamed her face, and Skye could feel the color surface; she always felt uncomfortable when people stared at her so closely. They had left Sally and her husband, Andy, after dinner and dancing. It was obvious Steve expected her to invite him in for coffee, but Skye hesitated pointedly.

"Thank you. I had a nice time too." Discounting the fact her thoughts had been with Jordan the entire evening, they had managed to enjoy one another's company.

Contrary to what Skye expected, Steve was tall and good-looking in a homey, down-to-earth manner. His mustache was an umbrella over a droll smile. He displayed an inherent sensitivity Skye found lacking in other men; his smile was warm and genuine, his laugh easy. She might even have considered seeing him again if it hadn't been for Jordan.

"There's someone else, isn't there?" He returned her keys to her open palm after unlocking her door.

Skye's blue eyes widened. "Is it so obvious?" she asked, feeling a twinge of guilt. "I'm sorry, it must have been a dull evening for you."

"Quite the contrary," he assured her. "I thoroughly enjoyed myself. I guess I should have known a gorgeous blonde like you would be spoken for." He used the old-fashioned term and openly admired her good looks.

"A gorgeous blonde like me?" Her smile was negated by a disbelieving slant of her head. "I won't argue, but you're good for the ego."

The masculine line of his mouth curved into a pleasant smile. "I mean it. If things don't work out for you with this other fellow, give me a call. Andy has my number." His eyes grew serious. Very gently he placed a fleeting kiss upon her unsuspecting lips before adding, "I'm very interested. Whoever he is, he's a lucky man." He opened the apartment door for her and retreated.

"Good night . . . Steve." She faltered slightly over his name. "And thanks again."

He turned and gave a friendly wave. "Good-bye, Skye." A conclusiveness entered his voice, as if he was aware he wouldn't be seeing her again.

The morning sky was a pale blue. The early morning fog had dissipated, and the sun shone brightly. A thick covering of rich green leaves was making its appearance on the trees that lined the streets. Skye was up and dressed long before it was time to leave for church. She had chosen her outfit with care, having saved the powder-blue suit for a special occasion. And what could be more special than attending church with Jordan?

Her Bible lay on her nightstand, and she reached for it thoughtfully. If only she knew more, she chastised herself, maybe she could answer Jordan's questions intelligently and persuade him of the truth. A fragile smile formed. Did she consider herself more capable than the Holy Spirit? It was a ludicrous question. No, she had placed Jordan in God's hands, now she must wait patiently and trust. It was an encouraging sign that he was willing to attend church with her.

She met Jordan outside the steps of the church. Again Skye was struck by his basic masculine appeal. The dark suit fit him superbly, accentuating his wide shoulders and tapered to his slim waist and hips.

His eyes followed her as she approached, his gaze as appreciative as hers was of him. Skye felt elegant today, like a princess in a fairy tale. Certainly nothing to rival Karen Kane, the model she had attempted to imitate that first night with Jordan, but lovely in her own way. The thought crossed her mind that if she didn't strive for inner beauty as diligently as outer beauty, she would soon be vain.

Jordan's arm cupped her elbow possessively when they met. "Did you have a good time?" he greeted, his gaze probing hers.

"It was marvelous, just marvelous," she said, sighing, then giggled at the flint hardness that stole into his eyes. "Steve turned out to be a very nice gentleman, but I think I must have been rotten company, since my thoughts were with you. In fact—" she smiled broadly "—it was so obvious, he told me to tell you that you're a lucky man." Tilting her head and patting her hair, she continued, "And in this new outfit I tend to agree with him."

Jordan laughed, but then his expression grew sober. "You won't see him again." It wasn't a suggestion but a statement of fact.

Without argument she nodded and turned her attention to others who were beginning to file into the church. When she happened to glance up, she found Jordan watching her with a look of unbelievable tenderness.

"I have an irrepressible desire to throw good taste to the wind and startle these churchgoers by kissing the living daylights out of you."

A flood of color flushed her face, but her eyes shone with a vital happiness. Jordan's gaze became obsessively attached to her lips.

The attraction between them was volatile, and flirting with the danger, Skye provocatively outlined the shape of her lips with a tip of her tongue.

Jordan paled, his gaze pinning hers. "Stop it, Skye," he murmured under his breath fiercely. Their eyes remained locked until Skye lowered her gaze.

It was so unlike her to flirt quite so openly; what was making her act so out of character? Before she could fully consider her actions, Jordan's hand slipped around her waist, and they entered the church together.

The interior of the building was decorated with lilies, which surrounded the altar. A large flowing banner was suspended from the rafters, hanging behind the altar. Its announcement—HE LIVES—was a reminder of the Easter season just passed.

Skye sat with the members of the choir in the front of the congregation and to the left of the altar.

The choir number was scheduled midway through the service, before the pastor's message. Skye was in the front row and stepped forward before the choir for her solo. Slightly nervous, she felt her stomach twitch with the first few notes, but as the song progressed she gained confidence, and her strong, clear voice rang through the church with a richness and clarity that was breathtaking. Her versatile voice had a three-octave range, and the difficulty of the musical score called upon the full gauge of her ability.

When the vocal presentation was finished, a hushed awe filled the church. As was the custom there was no applause, which suited Skye. If there were any appreciation for her talent the praise should be directed to her Creator; He was the One who deserved the glory, not she.

Brad and family found Skye and Jordan on the steps of the church after the service. The two men shook hands and chatted easily. Peggy winked at Skye knowingly while Janey skipped blithely up and down the stairs with her friends.

"It's good to see you, Jordan." Brad's arm was draped around Peggy's shoulders, holding her protectively close to his side. His smile fell on Skye. "Mom would have been very proud to have heard you today. You were great. I can't recall a time you sounded better."

Skye blushed becomingly. "God and I thank you." In her heart, she recognized she'd been singing to Jordan. The song was one of joy at the freedom and new life offered through Christ.

"I've been trying to persuade this stubborn sister of yours to let a friend of mine in the music world listen to her, but Skye won't hear of it."

Skye cast a pleading glance to Brad, but he quickly ignored the silent appeal. "You should, sis."

Peggy's apologetic gaze met Skye's. "You two leave Skye alone. Let her make her own decisions."

Skye sighed, grateful for Peggy's intervention. "Yeah, you two leave me alone," she remarked with a half-smile.

The men spoke for several more minutes while Brad described his new job eagerly.

"Are you ready to go?" Jordan smiled at her.

"He's flying home this afternoon," Skye explained to her family.

"Did you get my letter?" Janey wanted to know, leaping three steps at once to land directly in front of Jordan.

"Sure did, Cupcake," he used Skye's pet name for her niece. "I'm glad you and Samson like his house so well."

They bid their farewells, and Skye promised to stop by Brad and Peggy's later for dinner.

The ride to the airport was quiet and serene. Jordan's arm rested possessively around her shoulder, and when he tenderly kissed her temple, Skye turned and smiled at him peacefully.

"Tired?" Her small yawn prompted the question.

"No, content." It was so right to feel his arms holding her securely. Though another separation was inevitable, none of the agonies she'd experienced with their first parting remained.

She felt Jordan's eyes rest on her thoughtfully, but didn't turn to intercept his gaze. Gently the pressure of his lips moved across her hair.

When the cab pulled along the curb at the airport, the driver stepped out to attend to the luggage.

Jordan turned Skye to face him, and stared deep into her cobalt blue eyes, the tenderness unmasked and bare. "We never did have our talk," he whispered. "There never seems to be enough time to say all the things we need to say," he paused. "I know it bothers you that I don't believe in God the same way you do, Skye. Be patient with me." Slowly he drew her into his arms.

He'd asked her to be patient, and Skye realized that she'd wait until doomsday for this man. She trembled, anticipating his kiss, then savored the moment with all the longings of her soul. Jordan shuddered, his breathing ragged and barely controlled. He rested his forehead against hers, as if fighting for command of his senses.

"You go to my head," he murmured heavily, the warmth of his breath fanning her flushed face.

"Good thing," she whispered. "I'd hate to think I was feeling this way alone."

Again, he folded her tightly into his arms. "I'll phone Wednesday evening." His own voice was as shaky as hers.

"I'll be waiting." Suddenly she was free. She felt cold without his arms around her, and it was in a daze that she watched him pay the driver and enter the airport building. When the cab began to move and weave its way through the traffic, Skye suddenly realized she didn't know where he was taking her.

"Where am I going?"

The driver turned and, giving her a funny look, mumbled off Brad's address.

"How you doing, Sprout?" Playfully Skye ruffled the crop of short blond hair.

"All right, I guess," he said without enthusiasm.

"Aren't you feeling well?" Concern knitted her brow; Billy so seldom complained. This subdued behavior was very unlike the gregarious youth Skye had come to love and admire. "Are you going to tell me what's the matter?" Gently she began to stroke his head, as if to ease his discomfort.

Indecision moved over his young face. "I . . . I overheard my Mom and Dr. Warren talking," he began shakily, close to tears. "They didn't know I could hear them. They thought I was asleep. Dr. Warren told Mom there may be a chance I could walk again, but I'll need this new kind of operation." A solitary tear escaped and slid from the corner of his eye onto the white pillowcase. Embarrassed, Billy fiercely wiped his eyes. "My mom needs me to take care of her. Ever since Dad left, she's been so unhappy. She used to cry all the time—she still cries—but she tries not to let me know. I don't want to walk just for me. I need to walk for Mom. I'll be able to look after her then, instead of her looking after me."

Billy's unselfish concern for his mother brought tears shimmering to her eyes. "Then we must pray very hard, Billy. But most of all, we must believe Jesus loves you and your mother and He knows what's best for the both of you. We must trust Him to do what's right."

"Will you pray with me?" he whispered, almost as if he were afraid prayers were a sign of weakness instead of strength.

"Of course I will, every night, if you want," she promised.

The troubled face relaxed.

"If you're able to have the surgery, would you like me to stay with your mother? We could wait and pray together for you." Billy's sense of duty was so strong toward his mother, Skye knew this would help him.

A smile brightened his face. "Would you?"

"Sure thing, Sprout," she promised.

Later that evening, after Skye had sung and entertained the children, Sally joined her in the nurses' lounge for a cup of coffee.

"Dr. Warren has begun some of the testing on Billy," Sally announced.

"And?" Skye couldn't disguise the concern that heavily laced her voice.

"Thus far, it looks favorable, but everything rests on Dr. Snell's opinion," Sally explained with tightlipped anxiety. Elaborating on the details the operation would entail, Sally was interrupted by a volunteer.

"Skye, there's a call for you on line one." Joyce Kimball stuck her head around the corner of the doorframe. "I had it transferred in here. You can use the phone on the countertop."

"Thanks, Joyce." Setting her cup on the table, Skye moved to the phone. "I wonder who would be phoning me here?"

Sally slouched indolently and batted her eyelashes teasingly. "I bet it's Jordan Kiley. He's fallen for you, my dear girl."

"Hardly." Skye dismissed the thought with a wave of her hand and turned her back on Sally's wicked gleam.

"This is Skye Garvin," she spoke hesitatingly.

"Hello, Blue Eyes."

It was Jordan, and the tender affection in his voice brought a tingling sensation to the ends of her nerves. But before she could express her surprise, Jordan continued.

"Are you free tomorrow afternoon?" The question was abrupt; asked in a brisk voice.

"Yes." She moistened her suddenly dry lips. "I can't think of anything offhand. Why?"

"Good. I'll pick you up after school; wait there for me. I haven't time to explain now. I'll see you tomorrow." As quickly as the conversation had begun it was over. Skye turned back to Sally, her expression showing her confusion.

"Jordan?" Sally asked with a know-it-all attitude.

Skye wasn't aware of Sally's righteous gaze and nodded, deep in thought. "He's coming tomorrow but . . . but he didn't say why."

"This sounds serious to me," Sally teased, twitching her eyebrows.

Still thinking about the brief conversation, Skye didn't notice the dramatic scene Sally was enacting until she glanced upward to witness a paper towel draped over Sally's head as she slowly marched up the imaginary aisle, singing in her loudest voice the reprise to the wedding march.

"Here comes the bride . . . tall, skinny and snide . . ." Before she could complete another witticism, Skye threw a pillow in her direction and burst into laughter.

The afternoon beams of sunlight filtered through the window of Skye's classroom. Looping a long strand of honey-colored hair behind her ear, she stood from her position on the floor with the children and stretched. A warm sensation grew within her at the beauty of the unspoiled day. With the warm weather the children were anxious to be outside and rose eagerly when the bell rang announcing the close of another day. Within minutes her classroom was empty as the children exploded onto the playground.

When Skye returned to her desk to straighten a few papers, she caught sight of Jordan through her windows, walking across the school grounds, weaving his way between the children. Unbidden, her senses clamored at the sight of him, and she recognized anew the depth of her feeling for this virile man. His face looked drawn and tired, as if something were weighing on his mind, but the look they exchanged when their eyes met was anything but jaded.

He entered her class, his smile warm and disturbing. "Why is it none of my teachers were ever this beautiful?" he murmured.

Skye smiled contentedly, standing to greet him.

"On second thought—" his hand cupped her face and he peered into her eyes "—I may never have completed school if you'd been around. It would have been too tempting to flunk."

Unable to resist the temptation, Skye planted a tiny kiss at the corner of his mouth. More and more, touching him, kissing him, loving him, was becoming second nature.

"Are you ready?" his controlled voice asked.

"In a minute." Reluctantly she broke from his arms and withdrew her purse from the bottom drawer of her desk. "Do I have time to freshen up? I'll only be a few minutes." Her fingers rose unconsciously to her colorless lips before running through the tangles of her long curls.

"I don't see why you need fresh lipstick. I'm going to kiss it off within minutes anyway," he teased, the corners of his mouth curved in amusement. "But take all the time you need."

When she joined him again, she found him leaning against her desk, glancing through her students' papers and their still awkward attempts at letters and numbers. He straightened when she entered, but the drawn look was back in his eyes before he could mask it from her.

A feather-light kiss brushed her lips. "Mmm, that tasted good." His head drew back slightly to examine her trembling mouth. "I'll have another," he said, and with a diminutive chuckle, he tenderly folded her into his arms.

"How did you know where I taught?" Skye asked, still descending from the delight of his kiss. The question had troubled her all day. She was sure she'd never mentioned it.

"You told me at one time or another." He dismissed her question. "Or perhaps it was Billy."

She relaxed. Billy knew, of course. Yet she couldn't help feeling a little apprehensive. Jordan's call last night had haunted her most of the day, and looking at him now, she could see he was equally troubled.

"Where are we going?" They were halfway across the school yard before she thought to ask.

Placing an arm around her shoulder, he glanced at her questioning eyes. "That depends," he answered cryptically. "Why don't we go to your apartment first. We need to talk. We'll decide from there."

Skye glanced again at the uneasiness she'd read in his eyes. *He's going to ask me to marry him,* she thought, *and he's nervous.* An overwhelming surge of love rose within her. Just as she knew his question, she knew her answer. She loved Jordan, and she wanted his children. Together they would build a meaningful life. The differences in their beliefs would work themselves out. He wasn't a committed believer yet, but he would be.

Suddenly Skye was as nervous as Jordan and chatted all the way to her apartment. She put water on the stove while Jordan remained in her living room. She studied his profile anxiously, waiting.

"Skye, let's talk."

Instantly she moved into the living room and sat opposite him, her heart pounding wildly. She felt like a young girl nervously anticipating her first kiss.

"Yes, Jordan."

In a lazy, withdrawn manner he studied her, the pause lengthening. Skye had seen him use that expression only once before, and a feeling of dread came over her.

"I was happy to be in church with you last Sunday and listen to your music. It gave me an opportunity to record you without your knowledge. Dan Murphy listened to the tape and would like to offer you a recording contract."

In a hurt, confused action, Skye quickly averted her face. Closing her eyes to block the pain, she pressed her lips tightly together. How could Jordan have been so underhanded? She wouldn't have believed it of him.

"I'm . . . I'm not interested." She wanted to scream it at him, but instead remained outwardly calm and composed. Suddenly the living room became claustrophobic, and she jerked herself upright and stood before the bay window.

Jordan followed. "I don't think you understand what you're refusing." His gaze flickered over her as she stood, her back stiff and erect. "You've got it, Skye. Talent. Beauty. Appeal. You're superstar material, and I'll back you every way I can."

Skye looked at him with a sickening kind of disbelief and hugged her stomach, needing the warmth and protection her arms provided. Hanging her head, a numbness stole over her. And she'd thought he was going to ask her to be his wife. It was almost worth laughing over.

Jordan reached out to touch her, but she roughly pulled his hand away, her indomitable pride stalling the tears. "Don't touch me," she demanded in a sharp tone, anger wobbling her voice. "What's in it for you, Jordan? Twenty percent?" she spat contemptuously.

The muscles along the side of his jaw tightened and jerked in anger. "That's enough," he demanded roughly.

"You're wrong. It's not nearly enough." Unable to restrain the tears, they flowed hot and scalding down her pale face. Pivoting sharply around, she rushed to her door—remaining another second in his presence was more than she could endure. She could hear Jordan behind her and was caught by her arm and jerked around. The iron grip of his hands bit savagely into her shoulder muscles.

"Skye, listen to me," he ground out ominously.

Frantically she struggled against him, but the attempt was inconsequential against his strength. He shook her hard, until her teeth hurt with the violence. Roughly she was yanked against his chest. It was useless to struggle; he held her helpless for several minutes until the wild, crazy tempo of their hearts returned to a normal pace. Only then did his grip slacken to a less violent force, but he still didn't release her. His fingers combed through her hair, easing it away from her face. Skye wanted to fight, to jerk herself away, but she was no more than a lifeless rag doll with no will of her own.

"Dear God, Skye." He cupped her face, drawing it upward, but she stubbornly refused to meet his gaze. "I wouldn't hurt you for the world. Skye, I love you."

Swallowing the painful lump in her throat halted her outcry of disbelief. The heightened color of her face swiftly drained, leaving her deathly pale. From somewhere her proud anger responded.

"Sure you do." Her voice was thick with sarcasm. His lie slashed deep into her already wounded heart. Was he so desperate that he would go to any length to have her sign a contract?

"I deserve that," he laughed bitterly. "Good

Lord, I don't blame you for doubting." His thumb moved slowly across her cheek, tenderly wiping each tear away as it trailed down her face. "Answer me one thing. Do you honestly believe I'd take advantage of you?" The lack of emotion in his voice gave his question all the more significance.

Her instinct told her she could trust him with her life, but logically she couldn't dismiss his repeated insistence that she become a professional singer. Unable to find the words to answer him and equally unable to trust herself to look into his eyes, she turned her face away.

Swiftly he brought it back, the steel gray of his eyes pinning her. "I had to know," he ground out angrily. "I didn't mean to fall in love with you. You crashed into my life with a force that sent me reeling. At first you were just a challenge; the girl with the witty facade who was hiding from the real world. But the more I came to know you the more I realized that you were everything good I've ever dreamed a woman could be." His fingers dug painfully into her shoulder. "Don't you know what it cost me to make that offer? I had to be sure. Can't you see that? I want a wife, not a career woman yearning after the glamour and glitter of footlights."

Risking a glance, and yet afraid to believe the fragile hope stirring within her, Skye found his dark gray eyes gleaming with intensity.

"You love me?" she whispered, unsure of anything at the moment.

"More than I thought it was possible to love anyone," he expelled with a shuddering breath.

Her lips trembled, and she bowed her head weakly to shield her eyes. "I want to believe you, Jordan," she whispered huskily. "I love you so much."

The response for each was as automatic as breathing, and Skye was crushed against the steel hardness of his torso.

Against her mouth, Jordan murmured, "Trust me, my love."

"I want to," she admitted, and her voice cracked.

Framing her face with his hands, he raised her eyes upward. "I need you, Skye. My world would be a dark hole without you now." He paused, a smile forming at the grooves of his mouth. "Who would have ever thought a funny little girl who hides cash in her shoes would steal my heart so completely? Skye Garvin, will you be my wife now and for all our lives?"

Wide blue eyes stared at him with all the yearnings of her heart. "I . . . I don't know . . ." Somehow the words wouldn't form. It was what she wanted with all her heart. Why was she hesitating?

Dark furrows ran across Jordan's forehead, drawing his brows together. Suddenly the reality of his love confronted her, and with a happy laugh she threw her arms around his neck, hugging him close.

"Yes," she said joyfully. As the excitement began to diminish, her expression turned serious. "It would be the greatest honor of my life to be your wife and bear your children."

Locked in his arms, Skye surrendered as he hungrily sought her lips, parting them with a desperate need.

A burning question remained unanswered. Skye ended the kiss. "Jordan, what would you have done if I'd agreed to sign the contract?" Her voice reflected the importance of the question.

Jordan cupped her chin. Indecision danced across his face, twisting his mouth into a cynical mask. "Exactly as I said. I'd have done everything in my power to make you into the superstar you could be." He lowered himself onto the sofa; then his muscular arm circled her waist and he drew her onto his lap. Skye looped her arms around his neck, urging his mouth to hers. The moment was tender and serene, each of them absorbed in the magnificent gift of love God had granted them.

"I want to tell you about Glen," Skye whispered tautly, resting her head against his shoulder.

She didn't need to explain who Glen was; Jordan knew. His fingers began a comforting, stroking action down the length of her hair. "You don't need to tell me."

"But I want you to know," she sighed softly.

"Glen was a wonderful Christian man. Dedicated, sincere, gentle, everything a woman could want. We fell in love when I was fifteen and he was twenty-one."

Skye could feel Jordan tense, the muscles of his jaw constricted. "You were hardly more than a child. You couldn't possibly have been in love." He dismissed her claim.

Tenderly her hand explored his jaw, caressing and gentle. This would be as difficult for him as it was for her. But it needed to be said.

"We knew. Brad and Glen were best friends, and Glen was always around. Neither of us openly acknowledged our love back then, but we knew. Without a spoken word Glen waited for me to grow up. I know he suffered wretchedly through my first dates and the junior and senior proms. But he need never have doubted. In my heart there was only him. I never considered marrying anyone else. The day I graduated from high school he gave me an engagement ring. I think Mom and Dad were shocked; as far as they knew Glen and I had never so much as dated. Neither of us wanted a long engagement, but my parents insisted I attend a year of college first. The request didn't bother us. We had our whole lives ahead of us. Then Glen decided to enter the ministry and enrolled in a Bible Institute back East. We planned to marry the summer before he left, but my Dad was having health problems, so we decided to wait until that Christmas." Unexpectedly her voice throbbed with remembered pain. "I . . . I never saw him again."

"Don't tell me, Skye." Jordan kissed her hair ever so gently. "I don't need to know."

"I want you to know." She smiled, loving him with a ferocity that paled in comparison to the love she had lost so many years before.

"About the time Glen began his studies, the doctors discovered my father had cancer. It was agony to witness this robust man waste away. I sat with Dad at the hospital for hours, reading him Scripture, holding his hand, anything to lessen the pain. Dad had always liked to hear me sing, so I started bringing my guitar. I played and created songs to amuse him. Then . . . then we learned Glen had been killed. He was driving home. He'd . . . he'd decided he was needed here in San Francisco with me . . . the car skidded on an icy patch in the road and Glen was killed instantly. Afterward my music was the only thing that kept me sane. I spent hours alone singing out my grief. Up to this time my voice had been normal, nothing spectacular. But it changed. As Dad got worse, I played more and more. Dying was agony. But death came sweet, gentle and welcome. My new voice was God's gift. I could never exploit this talent. Since that time I've always used it as a means of bringing solace to others or to praise God."

Jordan's eyes filled with compassion as he viewed the tears that made wet paths down her cheeks. Carefully he brushed the hair from her damp face and tenderly kissed away each tear.

Chapter Nine

"Are you sure you don't mind?" Sally's eyes studied Skye.

"Of course not. I love Anne Marie," Skye quickly assured her, doing her best to conceal a smile of pure delight at having the baby for the evening.

"We shouldn't be late, and she'll probably sleep the whole time." Carefully Sally placed the sleeping infant inside the playpen that was serving as a substitute crib.

"It's fine, Sally, don't worry. Even if she does wake, I won't mind. I don't see enough of Anne Marie as it is." Her warm blue eyes shifted from the slumbering babe to Sally.

"Jordan's not coming, is he?" Again Sally voiced her concern.

"No, but he'll probably phone. He does most every night. You and Andy go and have a good time. Be sure and tell Andy I expect him to get this promotion."

"The phone number of the restaurant is in the diaper bag. Please don't hesitate to call if you need to."

"Yes, little mother." Skye mockingly rolled her eyes and eased Sally toward the front door.

"If she does wake, just warm her bottle and feed her. She'll go right back to sleep."

"Yes, Sally! You've already gone over everything at least twice." Opening the door, Skye ushered her into the hall. "I have your phone number, the doctor's phone number, the fire department's phone number and on the off chance I spot a UFO, I have a phone number for them too." The corners of her mouth turned upward in a teasing motion.

Sally giggled instantly. "I guess I am making a bit of a fuss. I really appreciate your taking over at the last minute like this. I don't know what we would have done."

"Nonsense," Skye said, dismissing the gratitude. "Didn't you say Andy was waiting in the car? Now, scat." She smiled, taking the edge from her sharp tone.

"All right, I'm on my way. We do appreciate it, Skye, more than words can say."

"Have a good time, and don't worry about Anne Marie."

"We won't," Sally promised.

Locking the door behind her, Skye tiptoed to the sleeping baby. Brown wisps of naturally curly hair framed angelic features. Sighing contentedly, Skye gently tugged the blankets around Anne Marie.

The two weeks had passed slowly. Jordan had been busy and unable to visit. Their only communication had been the daily phone calls, and these were often short, leaving them both frustrated.

Skye hadn't even been able to ask Jordan about a ring, and she wasn't sure how to broach the subject. It seemed petty. There seemed to be so much to say and so little time to discuss the things that mattered.

She hadn't mentioned Jordan's marriage proposal to her family. She'd rather they did it together, not that it was going to be any big surprise. Skye could no more hide her love for Jordan now than Peggy could disguise her pregnancy.

She curled up on the davenport reading. It was quiet, peacefully so, especially since John Dirkson had moved. Yet her mind raced with a thousand anxieties. Dr. Snell had been to the hospital to examine Billy, and the prospect of the surgery succeeding looked promising. But the strain of the unknown, the intense desire to do everything possible to help Billy and his mother, brought a worried frown to her forehead. Betty Fisher, Billy's mother, had been edgy under the strain of the uncertainty, relying more and more upon Skye for support and comfort. These were the things Skye wanted to share with Jordan. The need to express her own doubts and fears. She prayed continually for Billy and the success of the surgery, but her own burning desire to have Billy free from paralysis blocked her will from submission. She recalled the last painful days of her father's life and the desperate desire for his healing. He was healed, of course, but not in the way Skye desired. It was little comfort to a grieving daughter to realize her father was free from pain and cancer in heaven.

Thoughts of her father brought to mind something he had once told her years before. With a burst of energy she crafted a bright, colorful sign which read:

WORRY
serves no useful purpose
is of no value
and doesn't change a thing.

With a revived sense of serenity she taped the sign to her refrigerator door, knowing she would see it often and be reminded of her father's wisdom.

Feeling as if a weight had been lifted from her shoulders, Skye placed the kettle on the stove to boil. She'd just finished adding the tea bag to the boiling water when Anne Marie woke. She was startled by the strange surroundings and the unfamiliar face and gave a loud cry of alarm. Gently cooing reassurances, Skye lifted the babe from the playpen and placed her over her shoulder. Patting her back, Skye hoped to urge her back to sleep. While pacing the floor Skye happened to glance out her window and observed a black car pull alongside the curb. Smoothly

Jordan swung open the door and glanced toward her window, catching her eye.

A warm tingle of excitement raced through Skye, and she waved, her whole face brightening. Jordan hadn't figured on another visit until the end of the week, but nothing he did anymore surprised her. His job at the radio station, although he rarely spoke of it, was demanding and time-consuming. She had learned their time together must revolve around his schedule.

Noticing the baby in Skye's arms, Jordan cast her a skeptical glance. Skye watched as his expression changed from puzzlement to one of amusement. The lines at the corners of his eyes broke into smiling crow's-feet as he moved from her sight and into the building.

Skye was waiting for him with the door open, her smile one of welcome and pleasure.

"You surprised me. . . . It's good to see you." That was a gross understatement. Her heart beat urgently, anticipating his firm kiss. She wasn't disappointed. He closed the door with his foot and claimed possession of her mouth. Even with the baby in her arms, her pliant body bent toward him, yielding to the force of his kiss.

"That alone was worth the hassle of getting to you tonight," he said, his voice low and disturbed.

Dazed and happy, Skye blinked her liquid blue eyes, still trembling from his arousal. She was forced to draw her attention back to the baby, who began to fuss in earnest.

"Anne Marie Avery, daughter of Sally Avery." She laid the crying baby on her arm for Jordan's inspection. "I would like to introduce you to the man I love, Jordan Kiley."

Anne Marie cried furiously, her reddened face twisting angrily while tears rolled past her squinted eyes.

"She doesn't seem to be impressed." Jordan shrugged, studying her.

"Give her time," Skye teased. "She hasn't woken up enough to appreciate your obvious male charm."

Anne Marie screamed at fever pitch and kicked with all the strength of her eight-month-old limbs, fighting Skye's attempts to change her diaper.

"What's wrong with her?" Out of his element, concern laced Jordan's voice.

"Nothing a dry diaper and warm bottle won't cure," she assured him, bringing a bottle from the supplies Sally had left. "Here, warm this, there's hot water in the kitchen. Just set the bottle in a bowl and surround it with the water."

In her dry diaper, Anne Marie's cries became no less frenzied. Jordan returned looking slightly unnerved. The room went from blustering cries to restful silence as soon as the bottle was placed in the baby's mouth.

Jordan sighed in relief and relaxed his lengthy frame in the chair.

"You look like you could use a cup of coffee," Skye said, watching Anne Marie greedily suck at the bottle. When she glanced up a few seconds later, she found Jordan's gaze lingering upon her. His eyes were narrowed, expressing uncertainty, perhaps hesitation.

"Jordan, is something wrong?" she asked in a whisper.

His eyes cleared immediately. "No, I was just watching Anne Marie and seeing how very right you look with a baby in your arms." His look was tender. "We'll have beautiful children."

Their children . . . their child. A lump of wonder and joy blocked her throat; she felt almost like crying. The deep womanly desire to bear children was one she had ignored for eight years; now it surfaced and the longing to hold her own child swelled within her. Jordan was right; their children would be beautiful. They would be dark, like Jordan, but their eyes a striking contrast of deep blue.

"Do you want a cup of tea?" he asked, breaking into her thoughts.

"I have one. It's sitting on the countertop in the kitchen, but it's probably lukewarm by now."

The time he was gone gave Skye a chance to gather her thoughts. Children were something they had barely discussed, and there were so many other things they needed to know about each other. Perhaps Jordan would prefer to wait a few years before starting a family. It was another question to add to the long list.

Anne Marie finished the bottle, her eyes closed and she fell more than half asleep. When Skye gently withdrew the nipple from her lips, her tiny mouth continued the sucking action. She placed the baby over her shoulder to urge the burp forward by rubbing the arched back in gentle, circular movements. The release came, and Skye placed her inside the playpen, covering her with one of the blankets.

Jordan returned with their steaming drinks.

"She's asleep," Skye whispered, accepting the cup he handed her.

By silent agreement, they sat together on the davenport.

"Have you missed me?" Jordan asked with a coaxing smile.

She studied the steaming cup of tea. "You know I have," she admitted freely. When he placed his arm around her shoulder she snuggled closer to his side. A contented happiness stole over her as his body pressed close to hers.

"Then I won't mind admitting how frustrated I've been these past two weeks." The words were issued in mild exasperation.

Shifting her position slightly, she slid her hand around his middle and rested her head upon the firm hardness of his shoulder.

The gentle caress of his hand against her hair

was comforting and at the same time arousing.

"What's worrying you, Skye?" Jordan asked quietly. The pressure of his lips touched the crown of her head. "The last few times we've talked, I've felt you were holding something back. It's the most frustrating thing in the world to hear your voice and realize you need me there. Won't you tell what it is, sweetheart?"

A silence followed. Skye longed to tell him, pour out her doubts and fears, but she was afraid . . . afraid if he saw her lack of faith it would hinder Jordan's budding awareness of God. Dare she bare her soul again? She had left herself exposed and there was nothing left she could disguise from him any longer. Telling Jordan about Glen had left her naked; her heart, her mind, her soul.

"What . . . what makes you think anything is wrong?" she asked, her back stiffening slightly.

She could feel his smile against her hair. "Other than the sign on your refrigerator door, I'd say it was the hesitation and fear I sense in your voice."

Her arms tightened convulsively around his midsection, and she raised her face to look into the warm vibrancy of his eyes. Her fingers crept to his face, stroking the rugged jaw she had come to love so much.

"It's Billy," she whispered achingly. "His surgery is Monday morning. His whole life rests on the results." Her voice trembled slightly. "I'm so afraid. Does that make me sound like a terrible Christian?"

"No," he assured her softly, "it makes you sound very human."

"I am human, Jordan, and so weak. Billy's mother needs me to be strong, she's so alone and frightened. I feel like such a phony spouting off assurances when I am really a quivering mass of doubts myself."

Jordan's arms tightened about her. "My dear, sweet Pollyanna, when will you learn you can't carry the world on your shoulders?"

"I don't know that I ever will. It seems worrying is a part of my nature, but I hate it. Sometimes I see myself as spiritually strong, and I confidently want God's will for Billy no matter what. But I don't have the faith to honestly trust God with Billy's fate. I want him to walk and run and play like a normal ten-year-old. That's the whole crux of the matter—*my* wants."

Jordan's finger lifted her chin as he gazed into her troubled eyes. "But don't you think that's what Christ wants? I'm confident Billy is going to be fine no matter what the outcome of the surgery. As for recognizing our lack of faith, that's good too, because then we must rely on God, and that's what He wants."

Skye searched his eyes. This was Jordan speaking? This was the same man who had told her she was playing a Pollyanna game and wished to agree to disagree on spiritual matters? She immediately wanted to question him but hesitated. Trusting Christ was new to him, and she didn't want to rush his faith or make him uncomfortable.

"What time is the surgery Monday?" he asked.

"First thing. Betty and I are meeting at the hospital at six. Sally and a couple of other nurses are planning to come later."

"Damn, I've got a conference Monday morning," he muttered thickly. "What are Billy's chances for a complete recovery?"

"I . . . I'm not sure, but Dr. Snell told Betty there's a fifty-fifty chance he'll gain use of his legs. But he also said there will be months of physical therapy, if not years. This is not some miracle cure, nor is it a simple procedure that's going to make everything hunky-dory. Even if everything goes according to plan, it'll be weeks before Billy can even attempt walking."

Jordan's fingers laced through the long strands of her honey-colored hair. "Would you like me to be with you Monday?"

"Oh, Jordan, yes. But your meeting? . . ." She couldn't hide her desire to have Jordan with her. She needed him; for the first time in eight years she desperately needed someone to share her fears. Just knowing he would make the effort to come brought an indescribable peace.

"I can't guarantee it, Skye, but I'll try."

"I know you will." She'd been so preoccupied

with her own worries, she suddenly broke contact with him "Jordan, I'm sorry. Are you hungry? I didn't even think to ask. How about a sandwich?"

"Dessert?" His teasing eyes questioned.

"I have some peanut butter cookies," she said with a laugh.

"Cookies," Jordan said distastefully. "What kind of dessert is that?"

Skye blushed briefly. "The only kind you're going to get until things are . . . official?" She searched for the proper word.

His gaze grew warm and possessive, and he reached inside his pocket and withdrew a small jeweler's box.

Skye's heartbeat tripped over itself as she accepted the package. Her blue eyes locked with his as she flipped open the plush velvet lid.

"It was my grandmother's," Jordan explained, his husky drawl a warm caress. "I had the jeweler clean it and adjust the size."

Glancing at the open box, Skye gasped with pleasure. A single diamond set in an intricate gold pattern sparkled back at her. It was beautiful, more beautiful than anything she had ever seen. Simple, yet elegant; antique in style, but unique. When she raised her gaze, Skye was speechless.

"I knew you'd like it," Jordan said simply. He took the box from her, removed the ring and slipped it onto her finger.

Skye blinked through the wall of tears. "I've

never seen anything more beautiful," she mumbled ardently, her voice weak with suppressed emotion.

Jordan watched her intently, his look almost physical. In the next moment Skye was crushed against his chest. His mouth settled over hers, taking freely of her softness in a devouring kiss.

"Skye," he whispered achingly, "this had better be a short engagement. I'm not going to be able to keep my hands off you much longer." His mouth burned hers in another passionate kiss.

Sliding her arms around his neck, she rested her head softly against his shoulder until their breathing had returned to normal. She raised herself slightly, turning his face toward her. "I want children, I don't want to wait to start a family." It was a crazy thing to say under the circumstances. Before questioning her actions, she opened her lips and kissed him hard and long.

Jordan moaned and shuddered before breaking the contact. "Unless you wish to start our family tonight, I suggest we stop this torture."

"Would you like a sandwich?" Skye asked apologetically. Her actions weren't helping either of them battle the temptations of their love.

"No, but fix me one anyway." Jordan helped her up and gave her rump a solid whack as she rose. "And no more teasing, understand?"

She nodded, her face a rosy hue. "But, Jordan, I wasn't teasing about wanting a family right away. I do want children."

His look darkened. "Skye," his raw voice pleaded with her, "fix me that sandwich."

Opening the refrigerator door, Skye scanned its contents for something appetizing. "Leftover roast beef okay?" She glanced toward Jordan.

"Fine." He was standing over the slumbering baby, his look warm and tender. "Do they always sleep this peacefully?" he asked, his voice startling Anne Marie, who woke with a feeble cry. Attempting to correct the damage, Jordan began whispering reassurances to her while casting a pleading look in Skye's direction.

Skye grinned at him, her eyes full of amusement. "You woke her, you take care of her."

The baby cried in earnest, and Skye laughed aloud at the frustrated, helpless look Jordan gave her.

"All right, all right." She set the sandwich makings on the countertop. "I'm coming."

The minute the baby was in her arms, the cries lessened. But it was obvious Anne Marie needed her diaper changed; her blanket and her sleeper were moist and clammy.

"Can I help?" Jordan offered.

"Give her your hand," Skye suggested as she snapped the legs of the sleeper together.

Jordan's gaze rushed over her skeptically before his hand smoothed the rumpled mass of her unruly curls. The taut muscles of his face relaxed as the baby cooed.

"For someone so little she has a good pair of lungs, doesn't she?" He bent forward again and Anne Marie firmly gripped his little finger.

Both awake and alert, Anne Marie sat on Jordan's lap looking around curiously while Skye finished making the sandwich.

"I told you once she woke up she'd fall prey to your male charms. She hasn't been that content all night." She handed Jordan the sandwich and took Anne Marie.

"The kid's on her best behavior. She knows a prospective father when she sees one." He took a bite of the roast beef. "This is good."

"I'm on my best behavior too," Skye joked. "I know a prospective husband when I see one."

They laughed, but when their eyes met, they locked, sharing promises they were both eager to collect.

Skye broke the contact first. "How did you know my ring size?" she asked. The ring felt unfamiliar on her finger.

"I'm glad you reminded me." He pulled something from his pocket and extended his hand to her.

"What's this?"

"The ring I lifted from you the last time I was here. I needed to know your ring size and wanted to surprise you."

"Jordan," she said incredulously, "you didn't! Do you realize what you put me through? I knew the ring was on the kitchen countertop the last time you were here, and after you left it was missing." She flushed guiltily. "I thought you'd stolen it . . . what else could I think? Oh, Jordan," she sighed heavily, "you don't know how relieved I am."

A grimness settled over him. "I didn't think you'd miss it. I should have said something; I only meant to keep the ring a few days. As you know I got tied up and it's been two weeks." His voice was low and filled with self-anger.

"No, don't," she interrupted him. "I've promised to be your wife and with that commitment comes my trust. No matter what the evidence against you was, I should have trusted you. I'm the one in the wrong, not you."

A brooding look came over him. "You mean you trust me unquestioningly?"

Relaxing against the back of the chair, Skye gave him a full smile. "Always," she promised. "My faith came with my commitment to be your wife."

"I'm not worthy of this," he argued, setting his half-eaten sandwich aside.

Skye bounced Anne Marie on her lap and the baby's glee filled the room. "It doesn't matter. I love you."

Jordan's sober voice contrasted with the playful sounds coming from the baby. "And I love you."

Standing, Skye transferred the baby to her hip.

"I have something for you, too. It's not a diamond, but it comes from my heart." She left him momentarily, returning with a leather-bound book. "This was my father's. I want you to have it, Jordan."

He accepted the book, respectfully turning the pages. "It's his Bible." A troubled look darkened his face. "I can't accept this."

Skye didn't immediately speak. "After Glen was killed, my father tried to assure me God had another man for me. Bless his heart, it was little comfort then, particularly since I didn't want another man. I refused to believe him and built a wall around myself. If someone had told me even six months ago I would marry, I wouldn't have believed them." She rushed on before he could stop her. "I owe you so much, Jordan, I don't think you'll ever realize how much. There's nothing I could give you that means more to me than this Bible, but I give it freely with all my love."

Anne Marie quieted as Skye laid her across her shoulder. Jordan's eyes burned with an intensity that seemed to reach out and touch her. The pressure of his hand brought her down beside him. He set the Bible aside and drew her into his arms. The taut muscle of his jaw flexed before relaxing. The kiss that followed was one of wonder, joy, and contentment; lovingly his hand remained to gently trace her face. "And with all my love, I accept." Tenderly she drew his hand from her face and kissed his palms, then rested against his shoulder in a comfortable and familiar position.

The alarm rang early the next morning. Skye groaned and buried her head beneath the pillow, attempting to escape the inevitability of rising to meet another day. Jordan had left only a few minutes before Sally and Andy had arrived for Anne Marie.

"Was Anne Marie good?" Sally asked with a worried voice.

"Like an angel." Excitement burned within Skye; she could barely restrain the rush of words. "Jordan was by and . . ." But before she could explain further, Sally groaned.

"Oh, no, I knew something like this would happen. I'm so sorry, Skye, we ruined your evening."

Wordlessly Skye extended her hand, letting the sparkling diamond on her ring finger say it for her.

For the first time in all the years Skye had known her, Sally was speechless. "You're . . . engaged . . . Jordan . . . marrying?" she mumbled between gasps of amazement and undisguised delight.

"We've set the date for the last weekend in June, right after school lets out."

Impulsively Sally hugged her in a breath-denying squeeze. "I knew it the minute I saw Jordan Kiley. I said to myself, this is the man for

Skye. I did, I really did. This calls for a celebration, anyone for pizza?"

It was well past one before Skye went to bed, but her mind raced and she found herself unable to sleep. It had been hours since Jordan had returned to L.A., but the lingering scent of his aftershave permeated the air, almost as if his presence had remained with her.

Skye had explained to Sally at least ten times that watching Anne Marie had been a blessing. Because of the baby's presence they were able to relax and talk, something that may have been denied them otherwise.

Now dressed and ready to face another busy schoolday, Skye downed a cup of orange juice while the contentment and excitement from the night before lingered.

Thick fog, so familiar to those in the Bay area, misted the streets and clung to the earth. The weatherman forecasted rain, and Skye pulled her new spring jacket from the closet. Folding it over her arm, something fell from the pocket—it was the uncanny fortune she had gotten the day she'd explored Chinatown with Billy and her niece. With a bubble of unsuppressed laughter she took the small slip of paper and threw it in the garbage. She had been undeniably silly to have allowed a fortune cookie to have troubled her. Her trust was in the Lord, none other. The flash of the diamond ring caught her eye, and she

193

paused to look at it again. It was beautiful, incredibly so—a promise of love. She would never know a greater happiness than what she was experiencing this minute, she decided on her way out the door.

The whole day was like a teacher's dream. The children were well behaved, responding eagerly to the lesson plan and Skye's elated mood.

Betty Fisher was waiting for Skye in Billy's hospital room.

"Good afternoon, Sprout." Skye sat in the chair beside his bed. "Hello, Betty. Are we ready for the big day Monday?"

Billy nodded eagerly while his mother showed less enthusiasm.

"Dr. Warren asked me to come to his office this afternoon. He wants to go over the details of the surgery with me one last time. Could . . . could you go with me, Skye?" The hesitation in her voice showed that she really didn't want to ask, but her fear overrode her objections.

"I'll be happy to," Skye assured her quickly.

"Are you going to tell them, or do I get the privilege?" Sally asked as she strolled into the room, her eyes sparkling with mischief.

"I'll tell them," Skye said with a smile. "I think they're the only ones in the hospital who don't know." She cast a pointed stare at Sally, who feigned ignorance. "Billy, do you remember your old roommate, Mr. Kiley?"

"Of course he does," Sally interrupted impatiently. "Get to the good part, I've got to get back to work."

Laughing, Skye conformed to Sally's wishes. "Jordan and I are going to be married." She extended her hand to show Billy and Betty her ring.

Betty murmured her congratulations while Billy grinned with a know-it-all attitude. "I kinda knew you liked Mr. Kiley, Skye," Billy announced casually. "Every time you talked to him, your cheeks would get all red. Stacy McAlister's cheeks used to do the same thing when I was in school. That's how I knew she had a crush on me."

The three adults exchanged glances while Skye did exactly as Billy predicted.

Dr. Warren's office was within walking distance of the hospital.

"Do you want to wait out here, or do you want to come and talk to the doctor with me?" Betty questioned as they sat in the half-full waiting room.

"I'll stay out here," Skye whispered.

Betty immediately looked disappointed. "Okay," she nodded, putting on a brave front.

Skye was half-tempted to change her mind, but she couldn't always be there for Betty to lean on, especially since she would be leaving San Francisco in June. No, it would be better if Betty started facing things on her own.

The nurse called Betty's name a few minutes later and she rose, sending Skye one last pleading glance. Skye winked, lending her emotional encouragement.

After Betty had left, she scanned through several magazines that lay on the end tables. An older issue that was dated several months back caught her attention. The cover showed Karen Kane's smiling face. Skye smiled secretly to herself. Of late she felt she owed the model a great debt. Flipping open the pages she turned to the article and skimmed the contents that recounted the model's industrious career. The second page of the article showed several pictures. One in particular leaped from the page. It read: *Dan Murphy, well-known music magnate and longtime friend of Ms. Kane.*

Dan Murphy . . . Dan Murphy . . . Dan Murphy . . . the full-bearded man stared back at her while her mind screamed his name.

Her fingers trembled so badly, she thought she'd drop the magazine. A knot formed in her stomach and twisted painfully as she continued to stare at the picture. At first glance she wouldn't have known it was him; the full beard hid his features well. It was the piercing gray eyes staring back at her that betrayed him. The man she loved was a liar and a cheat. Jordan Kiley was Dan Murphy.

Chapter Ten

Two nurses dressed in green surgical gowns briskly stepped across the family waiting area. An antiseptic smell followed, but Skye and Betty were unconcerned with its offensiveness. Both women raised their eyes expectantly only to be disappointed as the nurses walked through the room without pausing. It was too soon. They both knew it would be hours before they would receive word of Billy's condition, but they were looking for a miracle, anything to end the interminable waiting.

Billy had been wheeled on the long stretcher from his room to the surgical floor two hours before. Betty had broken into tears as she walked beside her son. Although drugged and woozie, Billy had attempted to assure his mother and sent a pleading glance toward Skye. But tears shimmered in her own eyes, and she looked away, ignoring his silent plea. Skye had wanted to be both supportive and encouraging to Betty, but her whole world had come crashing down on her and she was as desperately in need of emotional strength as Betty.

Now the two women sat together, yet very alone. Unable to boost each other's confidence, they didn't speak. Unable to comfort one another, they didn't touch. Unable to smile, they avoided looking at one another. The nervous uneasiness stretched between them to a fine, taut line.

As time progressed, every minute, every hour, became a battle waged against fear. Skye read her Bible, seeking solace, but the comforting words only skimmed the surface of her mind. The hurt and anger of Jordan's deception blocked the comfort of God's words.

When a tall, blond-haired stranger entered the waiting area Skye felt Betty stiffen.

"Bill," the name was wrenched from her in an outpouring of incredulity and relief. She sprang to her feet and locked her arms around him.

Skye recognized the stranger immediately. It could only be Billy's father. The sparkling blue eyes and broad forehead strongly resembled those of young Billy. Skye's throat constricted at the sight of the two entwined in each other's arms, tears streaming down their faces.

"I've been a fool. Can you forgive me?" he pleaded, his voice urgent. "I didn't know about the accident, I swear I'd have come home had I known."

Possessing a strength Skye would never have suspected, Betty calmly related the details of the accident and the events leading to the surgery. The fear that had sparked like electricity between them only a few minutes before was gone. This was what Betty needed to face the ordeal of

Billy's surgery. Neither Skye or anyone else could replace the presence of this man, her husband.

The scene was poignant and tender. The two needed privacy to speak, and after an awkward introduction Skye slipped unnoticed from the waiting room.

The small chapel was empty, Skye noticed gratefully. Here there could be no facade, and staring into the distance she allowed the acid tears to fall, burning her face. She prayed again for Billy, her voice a hushed whisper, and for a long while afterward sat silently and meditatively.

"How could Jordan lie to me like that, Lord?" she asked as all the pain of his deceit rushed forward. It was the same agonizing question she had uttered a thousand times during the past few days. It was ironic that he could have been so offended by her small deception and at the same time be grossly misleading her. She couldn't trust him or his love. For all she knew he could be offering marriage as a means of gaining the recording contract. And all their talk about trust. Skye buried her face in her hands. If Jordan had any love for her at all, why couldn't he tell the truth? How could she have been so wrong about him? Perhaps the hurt wouldn't be so intense if she hadn't bared her soul to him. The truth she'd shared with him had been a measurement of her love. Jordan couldn't possibly love her, she realized with renewed pain. Carrying the charade to this extreme proved his avowed love could only represent a shadow of what God meant for their love to be.

After Glen and her father had died, Skye felt she would never again experience such deep emotional pain. Now she was forced to admit her error. No physical pain could possibly hurt this much. Straightening, she wiped her face dry and swallowed the lump in her throat. She knew what she must do.

The swish of air came from behind, indicating someone had entered the chapel. The tiny hairs at the base of her neck rose in recognition. It was Jordan. He had said he'd come, but Skye'd half expected him to lie about that too. She didn't turn around, wanting to delay seeing him as long as possible. The sound of each footstep advancing toward her was magnified a hundred times until Skye lowered her head to reduce the deafening noise. With her eyes shut tightly, she prayed for control and the strength to do what she must.

When Jordan sat beside her in the wooden pew, Skye jerked slightly with reaction. This was going to be worse than she'd imagined.

"I didn't mean to startle you," he whispered tenderly, and with familiar ease slipped his arm around her shoulder.

Skye couldn't tolerate his touch; it made things all the more impossible. Trembling, she broke the contact and stood shakily, her feet almost faltering as she left the chapel.

"We need to talk. Can we go someplace?" she asked breathlessly. Glancing briefly at him she didn't quite meet his eyes.

Jordan's gaze did an appraising sweep of her face and the tiny lines of strain about her mouth. Her eyes held a troubled light.

"The cafeteria?" he questioned.

Skye nodded lamely and led the way to the elevator, pushing the button to the basement floor. They made the descent silently, the only sound an almost indiscernible hum of the elevator. The large metal doors glided open and Skye stepped forward, walking directly into the cafeteria and finding a table while Jordan purchased two cups of coffee. Accepting the Styrofoam cup, Skye stared into the steaming liquid rather than meet Jordan's eyes.

"Are you that worried about Billy?" he asked suddenly, the charcoal gray of his eyes regarding her steadily.

"Not anymore." Her voice sounded shaky, and she was striving for a quiet firmness. "Billy's father came. I suppose you met him in the waiting room." She glanced briefly at Jordan. She wanted to memorize every line of his rugged features and at the same time erase his existence from her life.

"Jordan," she began shakily, clenching her drink

with both hands and avoiding looking at him. "I have something important I need to tell you."

"What is it?" His hands gently cupped hers, his voice tender and concerned.

The hypocrisy of his concern gave her the courage to continue. "I've done some soul searching this weekend and . . ." She hesitated. Bile rose from her stomach, and for a moment she thought she might be sick.

"I've tried phoning several times. Where were you?"

She wanted to watch his reaction when she told him, but was incapable of looking higher than the knot of his tie. How silly it was to note how the dark blue silk sharply contrasted the pale blue of his shirt. "The cemetery," she murmured, returning her gaze to her coffee cup.

Jordan removed the cup from her trembling fingers as her gaze followed his action. The finger lifting her chin brought her eyes level with his.

"What were you doing in a graveyard?" he demanded, his voice tight and clipped.

"I had to talk to Glen," she said haltingly, her voice barely above a whisper.

His gaze narrowed, pinning her. "Glen is dead. You can't talk to a dead man."

"Glen is gone, I realize that," she said tightly, hoping he would see the subtle difference. "But his love for me is eternal, just as mine is for him."

"Stop speaking of him as if he were a living,

breathing person. The man's been dead and buried for eight years. It's time you owned up to that."

She ignored his anger and spoke with a grim kind of calm. "I was kidding myself when I accepted your proposal, Jordan. There will never be another man for me. I've heard of women who can only love one man in their lifetime. I didn't realize until this weekend that I was one of them."

Jordan's breathing became heavy as he struggled for control of his anger. When she glanced at him briefly she saw that the color had drained from his face.

"I'm sorry," she finished weakly.

"I bet you are." The aggression in his voice aroused the attention of others sitting nearby. Many stopped to stare at them curiously. Jordan ignored them. "I don't know what has gotten into you, Skye, but by God there had better be a good explanation." His hands gripped her wrists, his fingers digging painfully into her flesh. "What was all that talk about wanting children?"

"I've always loved children. I guess it's only natural to want one of my own, but I could never desecrate Glen's love for me. I can't marry you, Jordan. I belong to Glen. I always will."

His eyes blasted her a look as frigid as the Arctic wind.

"I can't tell you how sorry I am," she whispered.

He released her wrists, dropping them abruptly, as if he found her touch repulsive. His face was rigid with anger, contempt twisting his mouth into a hard line.

His hurt and anger cut at Skye until she could barely breathe, the tension mounting as the silence continued.

"Under the circumstances, I can't accept this," she said, sounding pitifully weak and breathless. The ring slid from her finger, and she held it out to him.

In the beginning the idea of lying just as Jordan had done to her had been appealing. She could terminate their relationship and at the same time salvage her pride. But she wasn't deriving satisfaction from this deception and would have blurted out the truth had she possessed the courage.

An eternity passed before he accepted the diamond. His hand closed over the edge of the table and violently he shoved the chair outward, jerking himself upright.

Skye watched him go, her breath so shallow it was almost nonexistent. Jordan weaved around the tables with long angry strides as if he couldn't remove himself from her fast enough. A second later he was out of sight and out of her life.

I should be grateful he's gone, I should hate him, her mind screamed, but her heart refused to listen.

"Heel, Samson," Janey ordered, and without hesitation the dog returned to his mistress, his tail wagging and dark eyes eager to obey.

"Sit," she ordered next, and Samson willingly complied, lowering his rump to the lush green grass.

"Good boy." Big, floppy ears waited for the petting and praise. Skye lowered herself beside the dog and Janey, who was now lying on her back examining the sky with a piece of grass clenched between her teeth.

"Are you two dog trainers ready for something cold to drink?" Peggy asked from the kitchen window.

"Bring some cookies, too," Janey instructed.

"All right," Peggy agreed good-naturedly and joined the pair a few minutes later with a tray containing an iced pitcher, three glasses and a plate of cookies.

"Have a cookie, Aunt Skye. They're chocolate chip and real yummy."

"No thanks, Cupcake." Her appetite had been nonexistent for weeks. She ate only because it was a necessary part of life. As a result her willowy figure now bordered on gaunt, as Brad had pointedly remarked.

"When is Jordan coming to see you?" Blue eyes, miniature duplicates of her aunt's, waited for Skye's answer.

"He isn't," Skye said flatly, struggling to keep her voice steady.

"I thought Jordan was real nice. I liked him," Janey insisted before reaching for another cookie.

"I . . . I think he's nice too," Skye agreed tautly.

"But I thought he was nice enough to be my uncle, and you said that . . ."

"That's enough, Janey," Peggy intervened sharply, watching Skye anxiously.

Skye smiled weakly in appreciation. She didn't want to think about Jordan or make further explanations; it only renewed the pain she was struggling to control.

"Janey, go inside and bring me my knitting." Peggy smiled gently at her daughter. "Thanks, sweetheart."

Janey bounced from her position on the grass with the fluid grace of a young fawn.

"Don't mind Janey," Peggy said, her voice suddenly sober. "She's been worried about you. We've all been worried. I wish things had worked out between you and Jordan. Janey doesn't mean any harm. . . ."

Skye swiftly interrupted. "I don't mind, but I'm beginning to think the girl is ninety-five percent mother hen." The attempt at humor was accompanied by a feeble smile. Thick lashes fluttered downward to hide the hurt and regret while her voice revealed everything. "I know it's difficult for you to understand, but it could never have worked between Jordan and me. There has to be a basic trust and honesty between couples—something sadly lacking in our relationship."

"But I can understand how the whole thing got

started. I don't blame him for giving the hospital an alias."

Why did Peggy have to defend him? She was experiencing so many doubts herself. It had been wrong to lie about loving Glen. Two wrongs didn't equal a right, but she'd been deeply hurt and had lashed back instinctively.

"I do blame him," she said stiffly.

Peggy sighed, expelling her breath unevenly. "Brad found out something yesterday I think you should know." She shifted uneasily, as if uncertain she should continue. "Jordan is responsible for Brad's job. Apparently the company owner is a friend of Jordan's, and he phoned, asking him to hire Brad. I'm glad Brad didn't find this out right away. I'm sure he would have quit, but as it's turned out, the job is perfect for both sides. And I don't know what we would've done if Brad hadn't gone to work when he did. His self-worth, ego and self-confidence couldn't take much more rejection."

A replica of a smile touched Skye's mouth. "I think I'd already guessed that. After we learned that Jordan was responsible for Billy's surgery and locating his father, there isn't anything that would surprise me."

Peggy defended him again. "His heart was in the right place. You have to admit that."

Skye's fingers curled around her glass of lemonade. "Perhaps. But Jordan was playing God.

I don't think he would ever have learned to trust Christ with his life. His money could buy him anything he wanted. For that reason alone I know I did the right thing."

Peggy gave an exasperated sigh. "You're not making any sense."

Skye stood abruptly, impatiently. "Haven't you ever heard the Scripture about it being easier for a camel to go through the eye of the needle in one wall of Jerusalem than for a rich man to get into heaven? I think I fully understand what Christ was saying now."

Peggy's expression remained troubled as she regarded her sister-in-law. "How's Billy?"

Skye smiled, her first genuine smile of the day, a poignant catch in her voice. "He's doing terrific!"

During the past weeks Skye had carefully weaned herself from Billy. His progress had been phenomenal, and there was every indication he would walk again. Billy didn't need her anymore, and for her sake as much as his, she'd spaced her visits further and further apart. Whatever differences Bill and Betty had experienced before were working themselves out. From what she understood, they were working with a marriage counselor. For all Skye knew Jordan had his hand in that as well.

Skye changed into her jogging clothes once she was home. She ran more and more now, and a forty-mile week was not uncommon. Running dulled her senses until she was so exhausted it didn't matter what thoughts her mind entertained. If anyone questioned her desire to pursue the sport she explained that she was considering running a marathon. To prove her point she competed in the Bay to Breaker City Run the third Sunday in May. She'd made respectable time, and was encouraged. At least running had helped her overcome the horrible apathy she'd experienced after last seeing Jordan.

The overcast skies didn't discourage her, and she set her pace, attacking San Francisco's hilly streets with a vengeance until her lungs burned and her calf muscles quivered. A loneliness beyond anything she'd ever experienced over all the years she'd lived alone came to prey on her mind. Before leaving Peggy's that afternoon, Janey had insisted on showing her the freshly painted bedroom being readied for the baby. Bright daffodil yellow walls decorated with Disney characters met her. The bassinet was ready and filled with tiny sleepers and booties Peggy and Janey had lovingly prepared. Skye laughed and chatted for a few minutes, examining each piece while Janey beamed with pride. But as she left, walking across the street to her car, the tears came. They were a surprise then, and she quickly wiped them aside without Janey or Peggy noticing.

Now she understood. The reality hit her with the force of a fist hammered into her stomach. She would never marry. She would never bear a child. When she went to bed tonight and every night for the rest of her life she would be alone. There would be no Jordan with which to share the intimate details of her life, no Jordan to listen to her silly songs. Her songs. She almost laughed. How very grateful she was to her music. It had been difficult in the beginning, when she'd felt bone dry of any creative ability. All her efforts had been channeled toward presenting a cheerful facade. Now she was grateful for her time at the hospital, it helped fill the void. Sally had done her best to force Skye into the dating world and wanted to set up another date with Steve King, but Skye declined with the promise that she would, given time.

Completing her run, her lungs heaving, she slowed her pace to walk the remaining blocks to the apartment. The hot water of the shower soothed her upturned face, but not her heart. Without Jordan she would have to relinquish the deep womanly desire for a child. Peggy's rounding stomach was a knife twisting at her soul. The euphoric experience of being a mother would be denied her. She'd relinquished so much in her life, she thought bitterly: Glen, her father, Jordan, and now children. The pain was suddenly so intense she could have screamed. Instead she turned, rotating her body under the spray of the shower.

She dressed and forced herself to eat half a sandwich. Although she had no desire to attend the Wednesday evening church service, she refused to allow any bitterness into her life. Her trust was in the Lord, she affirmed aloud.

Skye was grateful for one thing: Jordan had never returned her father's Bible. This was probably a subtle punishment that served its purpose in the beginning. Now she was glad he'd kept it. The time would come when he would be ready to accept Christ, and her father's Bible would be there. She prayed that when he read it he would remember her fondly and forgive her. She didn't hate Jordan, she realized. If anything, she loved him more. The anger of his deception was gone; the hurt remained deep and painful, but that too would pass with time. It would be very difficult to hate someone she prayed for, and she often found her prayers centering around Jordan.

The church was quiet and peaceful, offering solace. So much had transpired this day; emotions, awakenings, realizations. She wouldn't hide from her feelings again as she'd done after Glen and her father had died. Slipping into the wooden pew, she bowed her head in prayer. It was true she must relinquish Jordan and the desire for children, but the exchange was a fair one. Jordan had done so much for her, and she would always be grateful God had sent him into her life.

The pastor's words cut into her thoughts as the service began. The congregation sang a few choruses, and then Peggy and Brad slipped into the pew beside Skye. The Scripture lesson was on Matthew nineteen. Skye flipped open the pages of her Bible to the Gospel.

"And I say to you again," the pastor began, reading, "it is easier for a camel to go through the eye of a needle, than for a rich man to enter the kingdom of God."

Uneasily Skye felt her stomach begin to twist, and she sent Peggy a confused look.

Peggy shrugged her shoulders, her eyes as perplexed as Skye's.

"To fully understand this verse," the pastor began to explain, "one must realize that the eye of a needle was the name of a gate, and it was possible for a camel to gain entrance, but first any cargo must be unloaded." He continued by making the comparison between the camel's cargo and our worldly goods. "Next the camel was forced to go to his knees."

Skye's attention was pulled from the pastor as Brad began scribbling a note. Peggy intercepted it and added a message before handing it to Skye.

"Speaking of going to my knees, would you take Janey this weekend? I want to be alone with my wife," the note read. Peggy's message was an added postscript. "I hope you're listening to the pastor, and before you ask, no, I didn't have anything to do with his choice of topic."

Skye took her pen and scribbled a note back. "If you two don't quit writing notes in church, I'll report you to the church elders. And yes, I'd love to have Janey."

She rose early Saturday morning. She'd have to get her running in early since Brad was bringing Janey to her apartment around ten. She followed her normal course, which offered a variety of terrains: flat, steep, curvy. She managed the eight miles in less than an hour; rivulets of perspiration rolled off her body as she stepped into her building. She wiped the sweat from her cheekbones before stooping down to extract her key from a small compartment in the side of her shoe.

"Do you carry your whole purse in your shoe these days?"

The words struck her like a physical blow, depriving her lungs of oxygen. She straightened, slowly.

"Hello, Jordan," she managed. She wasn't ready to see him again; she needed time to school her reactions, to prepare herself.

He was dressed casually in dark corduroy pants and a charcoal gray shirt that matched his eyes exactly. It was the first time she'd seen his left arm without the cast.

"Can I come in?" His smile was without warmth. "Or will that defile your love for your dead boyfriend?"

Her back went rigid, her fist clenched tightly at her side. "You can come in." Nervously she ran the back of her hand across her forehead before opening the door and walking inside.

He followed her, closing the door. "I'm returning your father's Bible."

She nodded lamely. She'd rather he kept it, but to tell him that would reveal her love. Instead she mumbled, "Thank you."

He laid the Bible on the table in the entryway and hesitated before pulling an envelope from the Bible. "Your niece wrote me a very interesting letter."

She searched his face. "Yes, I know. She wanted to thank you for the doghouse."

"This didn't have a thing to do with the doghouse." He expelled his breath angrily. "She said you loved me." A muscle twitched in his jaw. "Is it true? Do you love me?"

Skye felt trapped, she couldn't lie to him, not again. "Yes." The lone word was wrenched from her.

"Why?" he demanded in a low growl. "Why did you lie?"

"You *lied* to me," she shouted. "I don't even know your name. Is it Jordan or Dan, Kiley or Murphy?" Her laugh was harsh.

He sighed wearily, the hard line of his mouth tightened. "Jordan Murphy. My mother's maiden name is Kiley. I gave the hospital the name of Jordan Kiley because I didn't want to be recognized."

"Was it some kind of perverted game to play me for a fool? Did you want to see how far you could go?" Her voice was treacherously low.

"No, Skye—*no*." He plowed his fingers through his hair in angry reaction. "It's true I didn't intend to tell you at first, but I didn't intend to fall in love with you, either."

Her gaze darted to Jordan, but she couldn't look at him long without revealing the effect of his words.

"If you loved me then why continue with the charade? If you trusted me at all, why lie?"

"If you loved me then why did you put me through this hell?" he countered quickly.

She lowered her gaze guiltily. "I was hurt and angry. I wanted to hurt you as much as you'd hurt me."

"Does it give you any satisfaction to know you succeeded?" he demanded, his mouth curving cynically. "Once you told me the girl's name who sang at the hospital was Jane. You allowed that charade to continue because you wanted me to like you for who you were, not for any talent you had," he sighed heavily. "My excuse, however lame, is the same. I wanted you to love me for who I am, not for anything I could do to advance your career."

"I can understand that, Jordan . . ." she gave a small laugh that bordered on a sob, "or do you prefer to be called Dan?"

His mouth thinned with displeasure. "Either."

"All right," she said stiffly. "But why carry it to the extreme? When did you plan to tell me? On our wedding night?"

"I meant to tell you a hundred different times, but something always prevented me. I had every intention of telling you the night I gave you the ring, but you were so concerned about Billy, I didn't want to burden you further. I was going to tell you. Believe that, please."

Her weary blue eyes slid to him again. "It's more than the fact you lied. You're a very rich man . . . you . . . you seem to think money can buy you anything."

"It didn't buy your love, did it?" he asked, his voice softening.

"No." Her hands gestured helplessly. "It wouldn't work, we're too different."

"We're not different at all," he argued. "We share the same Savior."

The silence that followed was profound.

"Jordan," she whispered, almost afraid to believe what he was telling her. "You gave your life to Christ? You're a Christian?"

A hint of a smile tugged at the corners of his

mouth. "It didn't come easy. The Lord had to bring me to my knees."

Suddenly the picture of a camel going through the eye of the needle in the wall of Jerusalem came to mind.

"You're right about my money," he continued. "In the past it bought me anything I desired. But it couldn't buy me your love. When we first met, I couldn't believe anyone could be so completely trusting in a Superior Being. You were too good to be true, and I kept waiting to find some flaw in your faith. There wasn't one. Soon I found myself falling hopelessly in love with you. When you declared your undying love for Glen, I was defeated. I couldn't fight a dead man. All the money in the world wouldn't buy me your love. I suddenly realized some of the things you'd been talking about. I read your father's Bible, I even flew to San Francisco to talk to your pastor. I've been a Christian for two weeks."

"Oh, Jordan," her voice wobbled, tears of happiness brimmed in her vibrant blue eyes.

"I'll ask you again, Skye. I love you. I don't promise to do everything right, but I'll try." A humility entered his voice. "Will you be my wife?"

She floated into his arms, as if it was the most natural thing in the world. "Yes, oh, Jordan, a thousand times, yes."

She was crushed against him as he claimed her

mouth in a devouring kiss that seemed to blot out all the hurt and anger of the past six weeks. Instinctively she wound her arms around his neck, arching against him. When he dragged his lips from hers and buried his face in the hollow of her neck, she could feel the uneven drag of his breath. Clinging to him tightly, she closed her eyes while an overwhelming happiness stole over her.

"Thank you, Jesus," she murmured almost inaudibly.

Gently his hand caressed her cheek, then framed her face.

She couldn't speak as she gazed into his powerful face with all the love in her heart shining in her eyes.

Four months later Skye surveyed the dining room table carefully set for the Thanksgiving dinner. Mentally she checked every detail; she wanted this day to be perfect. She'd met Jordan's family on several occasions, but this was the first time they'd all gathered together.

Mrs. Somers, the housekeeper, was a jewel, and Skye couldn't have managed the large meal without her. The middle-aged woman had been with Jordan for years and welcomed Skye like a mother hen gathering a chick under her wing. Skye had felt awkward at first. Jordan didn't need her to keep his home and she felt at loose ends with so much time on her hands. He didn't object when she began substitute teaching, but more and more she found herself involved in their church. Their outside activities would be curtailed soon enough, she decided.

One last glance revealed an elegant table set with fresh flowers and sparkling crystal. It was Thanksgiving, and her heart was full of praise for God's goodness to them both.

Jordan had to make a quick trip to the office, and while she waited for his return she wandered into the music room to play the grand piano. Her nimble fingers flew over the ivory keys with unquestionable skill; if anything, her love for Jordan had enhanced her musical talent.

How she'd come to love this room of their home. Smiling secretly to herself, she recalled her first glimpse of the twenty-six-room mansion. Driving through the long driveway after their extended honeymoon in the Caribbean, the house loomed before her, elegant, imposing and huge. At first sight Skye felt a tremor of apprehension.

Jordan had come around to her side of the car, opened her door and lifted her effortlessly into his arms, prepared to observe tradition by carrying her over the threshold.

When Skye glanced at him, she discovered he was watching her reaction. "This is our home?" she quizzed softly.

"It's not as awesome as it looks," he assured her.

"I'd rather live in a three-bedroom rambler." Their happiness had been so complete during their honeymoon, and now she was faced with the realities of his wealth and position.

"I know. But things being as they are, will you take me as I am?" An unfamiliar quality entered his eyes. "Christ did, you know."

"Then I suppose I'll have to," she whispered, and planted a warm kiss on his open mouth before exploring the lobe of his ear with her tongue.

"I'm back." Jordan broke into her thoughts, walking briskly into the rose-colored room.

Skye lifted her hands from the keyboard, smiling at her husband as he walked into the room with a happiness that was almost translucent. "Listen to this," she commanded as her fingers flew over the keys in a melody she hoped would express her love.

"It's beautiful," Jordan said, his eyes showing the special kind of awe he felt when he listened to her music.

"I'm trying to tell you something, and I honestly didn't think it would be this difficult."

His expression sobered. "You mean that you're pregnant? Do you honestly think I wouldn't know?" Suddenly, as if the thought had come to him all at once, he asked, "Everything is all right, isn't it? You're going to be okay?" His voice was deep with emotion.

"Of course I will." She quickly allayed his fears.

Drawing her tenderly into his arms, he held her close. "I love you, Skye. I didn't know it was possible to feel this deeply about anyone. You've become my life." His kiss was sweet and filled with passion. "How long do we have before my mother arrives?"

"Jordan," she giggled. "Not now . . . later," she whispered, her voice filled with promise.

She could sense his regret as he gently broke their embrace. "Did you know I owned your apartment building?" he asked unexpectedly. "I'm in the process of selling it. That's why I had to go to the office this morning."

"Jordan, no!" She was shocked, this man had a habit of saying the most astonishing things. "When . . . why?"

He chuckled, as if he found himself very clever. "It was the only way I knew to get rid of your pesky neighbor. I bought the building and tripled his rent."

Skye's mouth must have dropped open.

"Careful, dear, someone might think you're imitating a fish."

"Jordan!" She could hardly find words. "Is . . . is there anything else I don't know?"

"I don't think so. Oh, yes, I hope the mechanic did a good job on your car. I threatened to have his certification questioned."

"You didn't?"

" 'Fraid so," he chuckled. "But don't worry, I'm

learning a new way to deal with people. It's called love, Christian love."

Her fingers lovingly traced the line of his jaw. "Sometimes you shock me, Jordan Murphy."

He smiled deep into her eyes. "Good Lord, you're beautiful."

She slid her arms around his neck and smiled with intense satisfaction. "Tell me that seven months from now. I'll need to hear it about then."

"A child," he murmured as if he was just beginning to fully comprehend this new life growing within his wife. "I have something beyond price; you, a child and God's love. You've given me everything a man could ever want."

Jordan's arm tightened around her waist, and Skye happened to catch a glimpse of the dining room table. Thanksgiving: she understood the full meaning of the word.

Center Point Large Print
600 Brooks Road / PO Box 1
Thorndike ME 04986-0001 USA

(207) 568-3717

US & Canada:
1 800 929-9108
www.centerpointlargeprint.com